A Deepe Coffyn

A Deepe Coffyn

JANET LAURENCE

A CRIME CLUB BOOK
Doubleday
NEW YORK   LONDON   TORONTO   SYDNEY   AUCKLAND

A Crime Club Book
PUBLISHED BY DOUBLEDAY
a division of Bantam Doubleday Dell Publishing Group, Inc.
666 Fifth Avenue, New York, New York 10103

DOUBLEDAY and the portrayal of a man
with a gun are trademarks of
Doubleday, a division of Bantam Doubleday Dell
Publishing Group, Inc.

Library of Congress Cataloging-in-Publication Data

Laurence, Janet.
A deepe coffyn/Janet Laurence.—1st ed.
in the United States of America.
p. cm.
I. Title.
PR6062.A795D44   1990
823'.914—dc20   89-35032
CIP

ISBN 0-385-26626-X
First Edition in the United States of America
January 1990

OG

To my husband, Keith, with all my love,
and not forgetting Bramble,
who appears in the following pages as Bracken

The Society of Historical Gastronomes is gathering for a weekend symposium on food from times past. Darina Lisle has planned menus culled from centuries-old recipe books, and the presence of the fashionable cookery writer, Digby Cary, has attracted a large number of delegates as well as the attentions of a television crew.

The inflated egos of many of the "foodies" cause an electric atmosphere immediately, but when Darina finds Digby stabbed to death with an expensive boning knife, the petty jealousies and professional pique take on more sinister meanings.

Many of the characters had cause to resent the successful Digby: spurned mistresses; eclipsed cookery demonstraters; a plagiarised author. And as the police dig deeper into the background of the suspects, more serious motives are revealed.

Darina, too, is a suspect, but it is her sharp observations and intuitive detection which finally reveal the murderer, though not before a second killing is attempted.

A Deepe Coffyn is an original and satisfying whodunnit, and marks the debut of Janet Laurence as a novelist and Darina Lisle as an investigator.

A Deepe Coffyn

ONE

The head gave Darina a baleful look. Its ears were pointed and a shiny red apple was clasped in sharp white teeth. Just so might Little Red Riding Hood have disappeared down the wolf's mouth. Poor, defenceless pig, thought Darina, I've dressed you up and changed your character; who would believe you've done nothing more savage than rootle round your pen. She placed the glossy head on its stand, then stood back to assess her handiwork.

The long refectory table almost sagged beneath the weight of food. She walked slowly round and considered the spread.

Mediaeval onion tarts from England's earliest cookery book were flanked by dishes of pickled herring. Pepys had been fond of a pickled herring. The huge round of spiced beef came from an old Melton Mowbray recipe; Darina could almost hear the guessing that would go on as to the precise mix of spices used. Still in the kitchen was Lamb Monchelet, an early casserole from the same source as the onion tarts; that would come in with a roast sucking pig and whole sirloin just before the feast started.

In position already was the Yorkshire Christmas pie. Darina eyed it fondly; it was her favourite item. A chicken had been wrapped around a pigeon then put inside a duck, which had been inserted in a goose, which had been placed inside a turkey. The whole parcel of boned birds had ended up in a standing pastry case, beautifully crimped and decorated.

Dotted around the table were small pies, flummeries, Buttered Oranges, syllabubs and fruit fools. In the kitchen, gently steaming, were Steak and Kidney and Quaking Puddings. The last major task left was the arrangement of the elaborate salmagundis, the formal eighteenth-century salads that would add a decorative flourish at either end of the long table.

Forty members of the Society of Historical Gastronomes were gathering for their second annual weekend of lectures, discussions and feasting. Would they be impressed with the food? Even more important, would there be enough? These were no waist-watching nibblers; these foodies had the capacity of the most voracious of pigs after a long period of starvation. Trip after trip would be made to the table. Every dish would be tried, every item torn apart, verbally as well as gastronomically. Its antecedents would be haggled over, its ingredients assessed and fiercely debated, its presentation probed for authenticity. And at the end, what would the verdict be?

Last year Darina had merely assisted in the preparation of the feasts; in charge had been a famous food name who had found the strain almost too much, and more of Darina's time had been spent bolstering her confidence than in actual cooking. After the learned and ferocious inquisition on the feast that she had produced, the famous name had required reviving with copious quantities of single malt. Never again, she had sworn; no appreciation of her food as actual food could woo her back for a second helping of such lively and searching criticism. After all, who cared if the flour for manchet bread had been finely sieved to whiteness from wholemeal or came from a packet of bleached white? The Society of Historical Gastronomes cared. To them, authenticity was inseparable from appreciation of taste.

For Darina it provided a challenge that was a refreshing change from the production of highly finished works of haute cuisine, the influence of nouvelle cuisine shining out of each turned carrot and richly reduced sauce; all for bored Mayfair hostesses, or pressured directors who would have preferred a couple of lamb chops and mashed potatoes. But food, it had been decided, must reflect status, so bread and butter pudding could only appear after Anton Mosimann had proclaimed it chic by serving his refined version at the Dorchester, and a grilled chop had to be rescued from bathos by a parti-coloured sauce and a carefully placed exclamation mark of fresh fruit chutney.

This food, Darina thought, looking down the table with satisfaction, was real food. She was resigned to charges of compromise over ingredients, method and cooking. And she was ready to defend her dishes. In fact, she quite looked forward to arguing over the impossibility of recreating the ingredients and conditions of eighteenth- or nineteenth-century food, let alone those of the mediaeval or Stuart periods. It was all to be part of the fun of the weekend.

The heavy oak door at one end of the hall opened and in came the chairman of the society.

"Darina, darling!" She was gathered into a close embrace then held at arm's length. She stood quietly and let Digby Cary sweep a lingering glance over her.

"I can't decide whether to eat you or your food!" he said.

Darina sighed. She had no illusions about her looks. To start with she was too tall, nearly six foot. Her mother was petite, a frail vision of blonde hair, porcelain skin and bones so fine men rushed to protect her from the unkind blows of life. No one rushed to protect Darina; they were more likely to admire the skill with which she changed a flat tyre or hefted a heavy box of groceries. True, her hair was blonde, but it obstinately refused to curl. How many times her mother had sighed as she removed curlers from Darina's head and found the heavy hair sliding straight down her daughter's back. Now Darina had abandoned any attempt at styling, and simply used a butterfly clip to hold it neatly back, allowing it to fall like farmhouse cream past her shoulders.

Her mother had also failed to find much merit in Darina's regular features. "Men just adore a tip-tilted nose, or little dimples, darling. I'm afraid your cheekbones are too strong, your nose too straight and must you stick out your chin in that determined way? At least your skin is good, really could be called peaches and cream, but I'm afraid grey eyes aren't at all romantic. If only you'd allow yourself to get worked up more often, they turn almost green when you do. A bit of temperament is what you need, darling."

But Darina had seen at close hand what temperament could do to those around you, had watched her father retreat behind a wall of courtesy, spending less and less time at home, not difficult when you are a busy country doctor. No, temperament was not for her.

She looked up at Digby—there were not many men she could do that with but the society's chairman stood out in every way. While it would take a mean-spirited person to describe Darina's fine figure as large, no one would hesitate to call Digby huge. At six feet four inches tall, with a leonine head, he dominated any gathering.

Through television, his face was as familiar as any film star's, and as attractive. His continuous battle with his weight had so far proved successful, the flesh that generously covered his big frame well under control. His personality was as overwhelming as his size.

He smiled down at Darina, exuding charm and bonhomie, his face breaking into a map of deep creases, the light green eyes twinkling with a warmth that cooled slightly as she slipped out of his grasp and indicated the table.

"What do you think, Cousin Digby, will it pass muster, cut the mustard with the members?"

The creases deepened into wrinkles as he frowned at her, refusing to look at the table. "Darling Darina, why 'Cousin Digby'?"

"I think it's so appropriate for this weekend, such a nice, eighteenth-century ring. After all, you're always reminding me I'm your only surviving relative."

"Now, if you'd allow us to be kissing cousins, the title might have some charm!" As she moved another impatient step away from him, he held up a hand. "I know, I promised not to mention it again but you look irresistible with flour on your nose."

He whisked out a handkerchief and dusted her face. Darina broke into a reluctant smile as he finished by lightly flicking her nose. "That's better," he said, returning the handkerchief to his sleeve. He held her eyes for a moment longer, then turned towards the table.

The Yorkshire Christmas pie caught his attention immediately. "So this is your chef d'oeuvre? My dear, I compliment you, it's a work of art." The note of raillery had disappeared from his voice; professional was speaking to professional. "And that boar's head is superb!"

Digby walked round the table, examining the pickled herring, cutting a tiny slice of the spiced beef and assessing its flavour with the care of a Master of Wine tasting a vintage claret, putting finger and thumb together in a gesture of supreme appreciation before passing on to the Buttered Oranges. "So sad one must abjure all such sweet creations. I would like to think everyone would refuse these seductive poisons but I have no doubt most will disappear without many giving their dire effects a second thought."

Every muscle taut with nervousness, Darina watched him travel round the table. Most of the tension arose from the weight she attached to Digby's opinion of the food. Finally he straightened his bulk. "My dear, I'm proud of you. I could not have done better myself."

Darina relaxed—it was no empty compliment. The chairman of the society was not only the author of countless cookery books, he had produced the food for a number of historical television series. "I knew I was right to get you involved last year and to press for handing over complete responsibility this year, despite the pleas for someone with an established reputation."

Darina allowed herself to bask for a moment in the sweetness of his professional approval. "It's been fun," she said honestly. "Thank you for giving me the chance."

As Digby continued to stand looking at her, a smile deepening the creases in his face in a manner beloved by followers of his TV cookery programmes, Darina's satisfaction in his praise became uneasiness. "Come and see the kitchen," she suggested, turning away and leading him out of the high-vaulted fifteenth-century refectory, behind the pierced wood of the serving screen and through a door in the corner. A short corridor led to a half flight of stairs, then, off another corridor, a massive door opened into an enormous kitchen. A beamed ceiling, dark with the smoke of countless years, and capacious dressers bearing crockery and cooking utensils would have gladdened the heart of any historical culinary student but struck despair into the modern cook.

From the depths of a massive Aga, Darina drew out a pan of steaming water filled with Steak and Kidney Puddings. Digby could do little more than assess their number. But he almost squealed with delight when she drew out the sucking pig from the roasting oven, its skin gradually turning golden brown. From a supplementary electric oven, Darina took out an immense sirloin and basted its flushed meat and creamy fat with hot butter. "Wonderful!" he said. "I'm only sorry we couldn't arrange for an open fire and spit; we must think about that for next year. Meat really doesn't compare roasted any other way."

Working at a huge pine table in the centre of the kitchen was Darina's assistant. She was arranging rings of various chopped meats and saladings around a mound of rice, the gradually decreasing circles of prettily contrasted pale and dark greens, rosy browns and warm creams climbing up to a centre crowned with a lemon sporting a large sprig of rosemary. Two identical dishes of salmagundi were being assembled.

Digby watched the deft hands inserting marigold heads amongst the vari-coloured rings. His eyes dwelt on the demure face, crisp black curls and high breasts straining against the white overall. "What an artistic arrangement, my dear," he breathed into the delicately pink ear. The girl blushed and dropped the flower she was holding.

Digby turned again to Darina. "I can see all is on course for our feast; how about my office, is that organised?"

Darina led him through the kitchen, out of another door, back into a corridor and then into what had once been the housekeeper's room. Glass-fronted cupboards still held jars of preserves. On a painted dresser was a small group of kitchen implements: a spice box, an ancient ice-cream churn and a small miracle of Victorian engineering that peeled apples. On the shelves was a collection of gleaming copper moulds.

A table stood under a high, thin window. On it was a typewriter surrounded by cartons containing books, papers, and a selection of long blue cardboard boxes of varying sizes. Digby opened the smallest, revealing six wickedly sharp kitchen knives. He took one out, looked around, then placed it on a small table in the centre of the room. He repeated the action with another box and then another, building up a display of some half-dozen knives of differing sizes.

Darina picked one up, hefting it in her hand, feeling the balance, then brushed her thumb over the edge. "What lovely knives!" she exclaimed.

Digby smiled in satisfaction. "The best German stainless steel, my dear, cold tempered, containing a proportion of molybdenum, easy to care for, wonderful to use."

Darina found herself laughing. "You sound like a commercial."

The knife was removed from her hand and carefully replaced with the others. "I am giving members a golden opportunity to acquire these high quality knives, unobtainable on the general market, at very advantageous prices. They should all be extremely grateful." He turned to a large packet, ripped open the brown paper and removed copies of a glossily covered book, handing one to Darina.

The Case for Pastry, proclaimed the title, in black letters against a colour wash of ornate pastry cases, small pies and tarts. In smaller print a sub-title explained the book was *A History of Pastry and Its Uses in England from Mediaeval to Modern Times*. Then in large letters followed the author's name.

"My latest offering," explained Digby unnecessarily, his voice modestly lowered.

Darina flicked through the book, pausing at the odd page. "It looks wonderful," she said honestly. "It's so detailed, how on earth do you find time for all your research? What with television programmes, newspaper columns and demonstrations, I'd have thought you hardly had a spare minute."

"Oh, this is the culmination of a lifelong interest," said Digby carelessly. He took the book from her, wrote on the flyleaf and handed it back. "To Darling Darina from her devoted admirer, Digby," ran the inscription.

Darina flushed. "Thank you," she said, looking as though she would have preferred to hand back the book. "I take it you are hoping to sell these to members as well?"

Digby propped a couple of open books on top of the piles he had arranged around the knives. "Autographed by the author, they should go like, well, like hot mince-pies." He beamed with proprietorial pride at the table. "I'll get the members in here tomorrow. If they respond well, we might think of making other items available next year."

"I'm surprised you've never opened a kitchen shop," exclaimed Darina tartly.

Digby grinned. "It's under consideration, my dear. In fact, how would you react to becoming a partner in the venture?" He took a step towards her, placed his large, well-shaped hands on her shoulders and held her gently, an uncharacteristically uncertain look in his eyes. "My dear, you know how I feel about you. And now I am a free man, no ties whatsoever, God rest poor Sarah's soul, why not let us become a team? Think what we could do together, we could take on the world!" The green eyes held her grey ones, compelling her to return his gaze, then he bent his head and kissed her.

Darina stood stiff and unyielding, hands held rigidly at her sides, lips kept tight shut. After a moment the big man sighed and released her, then his mouth thinned and his eyes narrowed as she immediately took two steps back, out of his reach.

"No need to react as though I was yesterday's fish, my dear," he said lightly but Darina shivered involuntarily at the undertones in his voice. "Let's not forget who introduced you to the Society of Historical Gastronomes and put you on the culinary map. Remember I can destroy reputations as well as make them."

Darina's chin came up and she returned his gaze coolly. "I know how powerful you are, Digby, and I've seen how vitriolic your pen can be but only against those who don't live up to your culinary standards. I've yet to see you pull down someone just for spite. You've just said the food meets with your approval." There was a touch of defiance in her voice.

He looked at her with a long, level gaze, then suddenly smiled, a bright, engaging smile, full of guileless charm. It dispelled the breath of menace that had gathered in the quiet room.

"How well you know me, my dear. Your reputation is safe for this weekend. But who knows what opportunities I could or could not choose to direct your way in the future."

"Oh, Digby," it was Darina's turn to sigh, "don't think I'm not grateful for what you've done for me. Or that I don't admire you. I think you're one of the greatest living cookery and food writers we have. I'm proud we're related but . . ." She halted, searching for the right words.

"I know," he said smoothly, "you would just like to remain good friends, eh?"

She smiled gratefully.

"Well, my dear, that's what we shall be. And, who knows, as time goes by, you may after all find friendship deepening into something more. But I shall leave the next move to you." He turned with quiet dignity and began to rearrange the books and knives.

Darina watched the slight tremble of his hand, tried to think of something else to say, failed and started to leave the room.

"Oh, Darina," Digby's voice arrested her, "I nearly forgot, we have a television team arriving any minute."

"TV?"

"Only the local network but they are very interested in doing a programme on the weekend. I felt it was time we raised the society's profile and, who knows, it could be picked up nationally." Digby ran a now completely steady hand through his mane of hair.

"And Nicholas has agreed?" Darina was astonished.

"Ah, Nicholas! We both know what our dear professor thinks about any sort of publicity. But I am the current chairman and I have made the decision. Oh," he added as an afterthought, "the TV people will want some shots of the table before dinner, you'd better check that Nicholas realises that."

Digby turned his attention to his desk, inserted paper into his typewriter, opened a file of notes, sat down and began to type. The conversation was closed.

Darina forced herself to shut the door quietly behind her, longing to yank it hard and dissipate some of the complex mix of exasperation, pity, guilt and dislike Digby never failed to raise in her these days. It hadn't always been like this. Growing up, she'd found him full of glamour, a breath of excitement, this cousin who was finding greater and greater success in a world that seemed increasingly attractive as she herself began to cook. For a time her feelings had hovered on the edge of calf-love but in those days he had taken little notice of his gangling young cousin, beyond teasing her over her first efforts at cooking. When had her feelings towards him changed? After her father had died, when his visits had almost immediately ceased? Or when she had met him again in London, after she had grown up and he was married to Sarah?

As she went along the corridor, by-passing the kitchen and climbing the stairs, Darina tried to analyse her current feelings towards her cousin. The dislike was easily accounted for, she thought, from his treatment of Sarah. But why the pity for this protean figure at the peak of his profession? She could find no logical explanation, unless it was bound up with the guilt she felt at not being able to develop her teenage feelings. But she was twenty-nine now and a very different person. Digby, too, had changed. At forty he displayed darker facets to his character than had been apparent when he walked down country lanes with the uncle who had become a surrogate father. If only Sarah hadn't died, was Darina's final thought as she passed through the refectory on her way to find Professor Turvey.

TWO

In the main hall of the Abbey Conference Centre, Professor Nicholas Turvey stood studying his clipboard. Neatly attached to its clip was a list of names, most of which were crossed through with red biro. The red biro itself had a separate clip at the side of the board.

The co-founder of the Society of Historical Gastronomes was extremely thin. Only the fact that he was also extremely tall prevented the sight of the two leading members of the society from appearing a joke of music hall proportions when they stood together. Apart from height, everything about the two was dissimilar. Where Digby had a head of luxuriant hair, Nicholas combed wisps over a shiny pate in a camouflage attempt that grew increasingly desperate. Where Digby's crumpled face oozed distinction from every wrinkle, Nicholas's verged on caricature: a wide forehead narrowed ludicrously to a pointed chin, balanced by sticking-out ears. And too often his hazel eyes lost the warmth that gave his face the look of an intelligent chipmunk and gazed out at the world with baffled rage.

As Darina came out of the refectory, the professor's face lit up. "How goes the food?" The chipmunk cheeks worked, tasting in anticipation.

"All under control. How go the members? Everyone here?"

The professor consulted his clipboard. "All but two. So annoying they're late, I should really be mixing with the members." Unconsciously, his hand smoothed the lapel of his green velvet smoking jacket, then lighted on the yellow paisley bow-tie like an errant butterfly before returning to pick up the red biro.

Darina took a deep breath and relayed Digby's message about the TV team.

"Television?" Nicholas's head came up sharply, his nostrils quivering, a wild animal scenting danger. "What television?"

"The local network apparently, and Digby says they'll want some shots of the table before the meal. Didn't you know they were coming?"

The little mouth pursed and white patches appeared either side of the sharp nose. "All this publicity, so dangerous. An article appeared in *The Independent* only yesterday. Did you see it? An interview with Digby, purporting to be a description of the society and this weekend. But did it mention me? Did it mention my work?" Nicholas snapped his mouth shut and took a deep breath. More calmly he continued, "What Digby doesn't seem to realise is that we could lose control of the society, the most unsuitable people could want to become members. Really, he has no right to go organising these things without a word to me. *Television,* it's too much."

And it was too much that Digby had left it to her to break the news, thought Darina, he should do his own dirty work.

"And suggesting they film before the meal, it's impossible, it will make us late, the food will be spoiled!" The thin shoulders hunched and the long body knotted with tension.

"Don't worry," Darina said soothingly, "I'll see what I can do to put things back a little. And you can give them a deadline for the filming."

"Good evening, Mr. Turvey." Soft country vowels drifted down the ornately carved staircase. Following them was a small, sturdy figure. Brown hair shot with grey was cut in a sensible pudding bowl, a crimplene dress in heather-coloured herringbone was stretched across remarkably broad shoulders. Brown eyes behind pebble glasses surveyed the tall girl and even taller man with quiet confidence. "So nice to meet you again and I'm sure the weekend will be just as enjoyable as last year's."

Nicholas held out his hand, a smile of genuine warmth relaxing his features. "Miss Makepeace, settled in all right, have you?"

"It's all very comfortable, thank you." Miss Makepeace hesitated, her eyes, clear and bright behind the thick lenses, looking beyond the professor. "I wonder, is Mr. Cary around?"

Nicholas Turvey's mouth tightened and his tension reappeared. Darina came to his aid. "He's working in his office."

The broad shoulders squared themselves, and for a moment Darina thought Miss Makepeace was going to ask the way. Instead her scrubbed bright face tightened, her grasp on a capacious bag of scuffed country hide fastened itself more securely and she said carefully, "No doubt he'll make himself available later."

"Why don't you go along to the bar?" suggested Darina. "I'm sure you'll find friends from last year. It's through there," she added as Miss Makepeace seemed uncertain where to go. There was another moment's hesitation, then the sturdy little figure wheeled about and strode purposefully through the door Darina had indicated at the back of the hall, a waft of conversation and laughter coming towards them as she passed through.

"Dear Miss Makepeace," murmured the professor, "such an unexpected gastronome. But how seriously she takes it all. Last time she chased Digby from session to session trying for a discussion on mediaeval Tarts of Parys, if memory serves me aright. She finally succeeded in nobbling him on the steps as he left. I wonder how long he'll manage to evade her this time!" The thought restored a certain equanimity, quickly shattered by the opening of the massive front door and the entrance of what could only be the television crew.

There were four or five youngish men, mostly burly and dressed in jeans and sweat-shirts, hung about with an assortment of boxes, cameras, lighting equipment and a couple of bulging briefcases. All these they proceeded to dump in the hall. Then they disappeared outside again, their actions neat and business-like. There remained in the hall a slight figure clutching a clipboard whose massive load made that held by Nicholas seem an autumn leaf liable to be blown away by the first puff of an anchorman's spiel.

She advanced towards him holding out her hand. "I'm Linda Stainmore, you must be Professor Turvey. I'm so pleased to meet you, I do so admire your *Survey of English Archaeological Sites,* it's my bible when travelling around." Slightly protuberant light blue eyes held his startled hazel ones with a look of piercing intensity. A cap of black hair had the gloss of Chinese lacquer, a designer knit jacket and cream suède jeans underlined the obvious; this was no research assistant, this was The Producer.

Someone dropped a pale grey rubberised tote bag on the floor beside her. "Your bag, I think, Linda?"

She gave it a brief look, then focussed her high-watt gaze on Nicholas again. "Digby said you would kindly find me a room for the weekend. The crew will film tonight, leave and reappear tomorrow but I want to get the full flavour of the symposium."

Panic hit Nicholas's face. He gazed around at the purposeful crew, still lugging equipment in. "A room?" he said. He looked at his clipboard, then at Linda again. "A room?" he repeated, his voice rising slightly. "Digby has said nothing to me. I'm afraid it's impossible, we are completely booked out!"

Linda seemed untroubled. "Oh, I'm sure you can find a little hole for me somewhere! Where's Digby? He seemed to have no doubts." Her voice was authoritative but at some stage Linda Stainmore had been told more things came your way if you smiled. Hers had all the charm of a sycophantic vampire but Nicholas proved susceptible. He looked at the little hand lightly laid on his arm, each finger finished in blood-red enamel, then at the blue eyes gazing into his.

"Well now." His voice squeaked slightly, and he cleared his throat and tried again. "Just let me have a look at things." He studied his clipboard.

Linda waited patiently, her gaze running over Darina and around the hall, taking in the portraits lining the walls, the painted faces anonymous beneath layers of old varnish, the carving on the staircase, the heavy oak table at its foot holding a brass bowl embossed with elephants and containing an immense aspidistra. Beside the plant was a pile of thin files emblazoned with the society's logo, a peacock complete with trailing tail sitting on a large platter.

The red biro was making some rapid adjustments to the accommodation list. "As neither Charles Childe nor Gray Wyndham has arrived yet, I can put them together in the twin-bedded room and make the other available for you. It's quite small and doesn't have a bathroom, I'm afraid, but otherwise you should find it comfortable."

"Wonderful, I knew you would manage something." Linda looked deep into his eyes again and a slight blush came over the professor's face.

"OK." Linda became business-like, dragging out each letter in a way that stopped just short of affection. "The room can wait, I'd like to see the food for this evening's feast."

"Of course." Nicholas was all eagerness. "Here's Darina Lisle, she's the author of all this evening's temptations. Darina, dear, can you take Miss Stainmore through and show her everything? I'll join you as soon as the last two arrivals are here."

Linda gave Darina a cursory glance. "OK, lead me to the feast. And perhaps someone can root out Digby Cary, I shall need him for filming the introduction."

Nicholas's head whipped round. "Digby's preparing his address for tomorrow. I'm sure I could help . . ." He tailed off suggestively.

"You are sweet." Linda tried for a helpless look, falling short by a couple of thousand miles. "But I think it has to be Digby; the name, you know."

"Professor Turvey has a well-known name," Darina offered.

"Oh, yes." Linda gave it the stress of a nanny encouraging a none-too-bright child. "Of course. But it's the food connection we need. Digby Cary *is* food as far as the public is concerned. And it's food that we are interested in, not really the historical side. Interesting though that is," she added hastily.

Darina gave up and led Linda into the refectory, the television crew picking up their equipment and drifting on behind.

In the reception hall, Nicholas Turvey attempted to control rising bile. Digby, Digby, it was always Digby. For a moment there he had thought this attractive young producer had been charmed by himself, then Digby's name had come up, its incantation as potent as his actual persona. And when the name was made flesh, any impression he, Nicholas, had made on her would melt as easily as *gelato* in Italian sun. For a brief moment the clouds of jealousy parted and he wondered with an academic's incisive curiosity when it was that admiration, respect and liking for Digby Cary had turned to corrosive envy and eventually to deep dislike. What had the big man done?

Everything, his frustrated soul silently shouted. This weekend symposium, for instance. Hadn't it been Nicholas's idea in the first place? And hadn't the first one proved a triumphant success? Why, then, should Digby's ideas have been allowed to oust his for this second weekend? And all this publicity; he could see clearly who was being featured as the leading light of the Society of Historical Gastronomes, the one and only begetter of its proceedings. And it wasn't fair. Nicholas trembled with hate and jealous rage.

"Evening, Professor, are you signing us in? Sorry I'm late, things held me up, I'm afraid." A tall man had come through the big oak front door, left open by the television crew to the soft, early autumn evening.

Nicholas relaxed and came forward with a smile of welcome only slightly tinged with malice. "Wyndham, dear fellow, so glad you could make it. Working hard on the book, no doubt; how's the magnum opus coming?"

"It's coming," said the newcomer briefly.

"And who is this?" A playful note entered Nicholas's voice as he looked down towards the latest arrival's knees.

Standing quietly beside the long legs was a dog. To the uninitiated he resembled nothing so much as a walking hearthrug of a particularly attractive shade of reddish brown with an intelligent, sharp head finished with floppy ears tipped with black. At the other end of the hearthrug a feathery plume, also tipped with black, waved softly as topaz eyes fixed themselves on the professor's.

He held out a hand. The dog approached and sniffed it.

"Ah," said its master, "this is Bracken. I should have checked whether dogs are allowed, but if necessary he can sleep in the car, he goes everywhere with me."

"I'm sure we can find a suitable place for him." Nicholas was quite won over by the way the dog rubbed his head against his leg, looking up at him with soft, pleading eyes. Then he recalled the change he had had to make to the accommodation arrangements. "But I'm afraid I have had to put you in with another symposiast."

"As long as you can find room for this fellow, I don't mind where I sleep." He started to say something else but was interrupted by a voice from the front door declaring in tones that nicely mixed aggravation, self-pity and boyish charm, "This has to be the most difficult place to find you could possibly have chosen!"

Perhaps it was the suddenness of the interruption, or the slightly high pitch of the voice, or the way a hold-all was thrown into the hall before the speaker followed carrying a hanging bag over his arm; whatever, the dog Bracken turned, tensing in every muscle, his ears pricking forward, his tail held straight out. Then a low and menacing growl came from deep in his throat.

The owner of the hold-all took a step back. "I say, he's going to attack me, keep him off, keep him off." His voice rose in a terrified crescendo.

The dog advanced a couple of paces and bared his teeth, the growl rumbling through his body with increasing intensity. But any more overt aggression was prevented by his master grabbing his collar and holding him back. "I'm sorry," he said to the man cringing against the outer door. "If you'll move away, I'll take him out to the car."

Passage was quickly cleared and the dog led out, twisting his head back and barking furiously as he was force-marched past the object of his aggression.

Nicholas Turvey came forward, his hand trembling slightly. "You must be Charles Childe," he said. "Do come in."

With a nervous glance out into the darkening driveway where protesting barks could still be heard, Charles Childe picked up his hold-all and advanced into the body of the hall, his pale blue eyes widened in fear. He put the case down again and ran a none too steady hand through longish fair hair, then closed his eyes for a moment, dark lashes sweeping his cheeks. Waiting for him to recover his equilibrium, Nicholas wondered inconsequentially whether the lashes could be anything other than natural. Then their curving length swept upwards again and a smile of considered charm was directed at him, its owner once more in command of himself.

"What a brute! How could he be allowed loose! And in a public place! Surely there must be a law?"

"Sorry about that," said the dog's owner, reappearing, "I don't know what got into him, he never normally goes for people." He looked at the still-shaken man more closely. "Have you had trouble with dogs before?"

"If you mean have I been the subject of unprovoked attacks, yes! Actually, I can't stand dogs, they terrify me, always have ever since I was bitten by an Alsatian as a child."

"That's it, then. Dogs always know. They're reacting to your insecurity, fear and dislike."

"You're saying it's *my* fault?" Outrage took his voice into a higher register.

" 'Fraid so," said the other man easily, "but don't worry, I'll see

he's kept out of your way. Gray Wyndham," he added, holding out
his hand.

After a moment's hesitation, the other took it in a limp grip.
"Charles Childe," he returned.

"Well, now," Nicholas broke in, eager to get over and done with
what loomed as an increasingly distasteful task, "how lucky you both
arrived together. You will be sharing a room."

Dismay crossed the blond man's face. "Not with the dog?"

"No, no, dear fellow," exclaimed Nicholas hastily, "that will be
found a home elsewhere, I assure you."

He eyed the two symposiasts nervously. Really, the whole thing
was most unfortunate. One of the attractive points of the weekend
had been that no one need share a room. And it was all Digby's fault,
he thought with another spurt of anger against the society's chairman. If Digby hadn't offered that TV producer accommodation, he
wouldn't have had to put these two together. Quite apart from the
dog incident, they really looked most unlikely room-mates.

Charles Childe was medium-sized and dapper in a soft tweed
jacket of a far from traditional cut that Nicholas had no way of
recognising was by Giorgio Armani, cream trousers with unpressed
pleats gathered into his waistband, and a loose-weave coffee-col-
oured shirt sporting a knitted silk tie. He could have stepped from
the pages of a glossy magazine; even his features had the clean-cut
charm of a model.

Gray Wyndham was casualness itself. Not quite as tall as Nicholas, he still towered over the other man. His brown hair waved unti-
dily around a large head and his regular features were obscured by a
beard that, though neatly trimmed, added to a general appearance of
shagginess. From the wealth of hair emerged a strong, slightly
crooked nose and brown eyes with pouches of loose flesh below
them. A well-cut but ancient light tweed jacket and cavalry twill
trousers, both in the most traditional of styles, covered a lean body.

"Well," Nicholas galvanised himself into activity, "let me show you
to your room."

Both men picked up their cases and allowed themselves to be led
upstairs.

The Abbey Conference Centre had as its core an Elizabethan

residence created out of a disestablished abbey. A chequered history
of ownership had culminated some twenty years previously in its
being acquired by a business consortium and set up as a conference
centre. The large reception rooms took easily to their new roles as
bar, dining, lounge and meeting rooms. Additional accommodation
had been made available in a discreet annexe connected to the main
building by a covered way, and an efficient staff provided all facilities
and services.

Nicholas led the way to a large room on the left of the first-floor
landing, at the front of the old house. It was very large. Two single
beds clung together like children lost in a desert. Against a far wall
stood a modern, veneered wardrobe. Within hailing distance was a
dressing table in similar style. A couple of singularly uncomfortable-
looking armchairs flanked a spindly-legged coffee table by the window. From a large plaster rose in the centre of the curlicued ceiling
hung a long flex sporting an orange lampshade.

Charles Childe gave a neat little shudder. "Whoever decorated
this room would use wild salmon for fish cakes!"

"Seventeenth-century plaster-work!" said Gray Wyndham.

Nicholas nodded happily. "One of Cromwell's supporters laid out
a large amount of ill-gotten gains in the time of the Commonwealth."

Gray's interest quickened. "I look forward to seeing the rest of the
place. What's the form? Do we have papers tonight?"

"Ah, no; tonight we eat! A buffet has been prepared of dishes
from various periods of history. The idea is to discuss each dish,
what it represents as well as what it is, maybe comment on differ-
ences between the way it would have been made and how it has had
to be prepared today, that sort of thing. The papers start tomorrow.
Sorry, I should have given you a programme as you arrived, the little
commotion deflected me. There's a pile of them on the table by the
stairs, pick one up when you come down."

Nicholas left the room.

Gray Wyndham slung his bag on one of the beds and unzipped it.
Charles Childe placed his bags carefully on the floor and surveyed
his unexpected room-mate. "You don't look my idea of a gastronome,
what's brought you to this weekend of gluttony?"

The other man looked amused. "Gluttony? I thought it was to be a
series of learned dissertations on the history of food!"

"From what I hear, that's just an excuse for eating. That's what I've come for. I own a restaurant," he added, sitting in one of the armchairs, carefully placing one knee over the other, adjusting the leg of his trousers and waiting for a reaction to his statement.

"Serving ancient dishes?" said Gray Wyndham, efficiently stowing away the modest contents of his bag.

"Well, I'm thinking one or two traditional dishes, suitably adapted for modern tastes, might be a good idea." Charles twisted his head to address his remarks to the other's back as Gray threw pants and socks into a drawer. "I feel nouvelle cuisine is well and truly over, customers now want value for money. Especially mine. Lots of them are actors, you see, coming in after the show, absolutely *starving*. I was an actor myself, you know." Once again he paused for his audience's reaction.

"Were you?" It was not an encouraging response and Charles wilted slightly.

Gray Wyndham shut the drawer, checked his bag was empty, flung it on top of the wardrobe, looked at the figure in the armchair and relented. "Been open long?" he asked.

Charles revived. "Only a few months. It's such an exciting venture. Of course, it takes time to build up business, but we had Digby Cary in the other day. That's why I'm here, really—he was telling me all about the weekend, made it sound so interesting. Now, if he gives us a good write-up in his restaurant column, we're made."

He had finally captured his audience's full attention.

"Digby Cary?" the other man said slowly. "You mean he's involved in this eat-in?"

"Oh, yes, didn't you know? He's one of the leading lights." Charles chattered happily on, explaining the great man's involvement, his inspirational leadership, his scholarship. "And he has this wonderful ability to attract really influential people. Some of the really *important* people in the food world should be here this weekend. Now, if I can only get some of them to my restaurant . . ." He tailed off as the rigidity of the other man's posture struck him. "Something wrong?" he asked.

"I'm going down to see about my dog," said Gray shortly. "See you later." He swung out of the room without another word.

"Suit yourself," murmured Charles to himself as the door crashed to. Really, some people. He got up, unfastened his bags and started carefully unpacking his clothes, wondering enjoyably what would be most suitable to change into for dinner.

THREE

Linda was directing her cameramen in the refectory. "Right, Derek, panning shot of table, left to right, overview of entire feast. Darina, darling, what are these holes in the arrangement for? Can we fill in the missing items?"

The light blue eyes gazed intensely into Darina's grey ones as the timing of the meal was explained to her.

"So, what you are saying is we can't shoot all the food until just before dinner, right? OK." Once again the *O* and *K* were drawn out. She pushed her hand underneath the heavy fringe, holding the black hair up from an unexpectedly short forehead, and surveyed the scene again, her other hand on the hip of the cream suède jeans. Darina did not know whether she was more envious of the trousers or the slim legs they encased like gloves on a surgeon's hand. Everyone waited.

"Right, close-up of that pie thing, what's in it, darling?"

The contents of the pie were detailed. Linda's eyes bulged ever so slightly. "Amazing!" she said faintly. "Got that shot, Derek? Right, now that horrendous joint." She pointed to the spiced beef. "Sorry, darling," she said carelessly to Darina, "I'm sure it's quite delicious but when one's a vegetarian, that sort of thing does knock one back a bit."

She went forward and stood next to Derek, hand on his shoulder, and whispered into his ear. He nodded and pulled the boar's head closer till it appeared to be leering at the beef, then aimed his camera in a shot that seemed to go on forever before the trigger was finally released.

Linda moved round the table, minutely shifting a dish here, arranging a serving spoon there. Her page-boy cut bobbed round the pale face, the high cheekbones catching the powerful lights that had been erected; her scarlet lips moved, outlining a series of instructions only she could hear. The technicians stood, cameras hefted on shoulders, patiently waiting for the next shot.

"Right, everyone, where's Digby? Darina, darling, get that divine man, I want him to talk about the food. John, shot of Digby with food, me asking questions, right?"

As Darina left the room, she saw Linda glance round, locate a mirror and make straight for it. The scarlet-tipped hand adjusted the silk scarf at the neck of her Escada shirt, a pink tongue delicately moistened the already shiny lips. Darina hoped that Nicholas would not come in before filming had finished.

In the housekeeper's room, Digby was clipping together sheets of typescript. As Darina entered, he put the top copy beside his machine and the set of carbons in a folder containing others and pushed it beneath a pile of files and papers.

"Digby, the TV people want you to come and record a discussion on the food."

Digby smiled at her, a Cheshire cat smile that lingered on his features. "Of course, darling Darina, I'll be there sooner than thought." He switched off the typewriter and picked up his jacket from the back of the chair.

"Is your address finished?" Darina asked as he shrugged his large shoulders into the immaculately tailored linen.

"My address?" He shot her a sparkling look; like sunshine reflected off water, it betrayed nothing of what was going on underneath. "That's for later, I've been writing my restaurant column. Deadlines, you know, my dear, it has to catch tomorrow morning's mail."

He flashed another Cheshire cat grin and strode out of the room. Darina followed slowly, reluctant to return to the overheated refectory and listen to Digby's polished phrases giving an exposition of the aims of the weekend. It was time to check the beef, she decided.

As she opened the door to the kitchen, an excited dog streaked down the corridor, rushed up and cavorted round her, giving pleased barks. Darina liked dogs. She crouched down and fondled the thick fur behind his ears, pushing away the head that attempted to sniff deeply at her most intimate parts. He tried to lick her face instead.

"Bracken!" came a stern voice. The dog took no notice but Darina stood up and turned towards the bearded figure that advanced towards them. "I'm sorry," he said, "I'm afraid he's woefully badly behaved. He was a waif and stray and is pathetically grateful for love and attention. My poor attempts at discipline have totally failed."

"He's gorgeous! Do you think he'd like something to eat?"

"It's OK, thanks, I have his food with me." He indicated the large basket under his arm filled with dog food and bowls. "What I would be most grateful for is if you could show me somewhere he could sleep. Nicholas Turvey said there might be an odd room down here where we could put his basket."

Darina thought for a moment then opened a door opposite the kitchen, revealing a glory hole stuffed with odd boxes, bits of old equipment, vases and flower arranging items and an enormous boiler. "It's not exactly the Ritz but it's warm and he won't be disturbed here."

The basket was put on the floor, the bowls and food removed and his rug shaken and replaced. Bracken sniffed around, got inside, circled several times, then sank down with a deep sigh, resting his long head on the rim and looking up at his master with resignation in his brown eyes.

Darina looked at the tin. "Do you want an opener? And how about some water? Bring him into the kitchen."

She led the way across the corridor, Bracken joyfully following. Once in the kitchen he found a multitude of smells to investigate and several titbits that needed hoovering up from the floor. Darina found some chopped meat left over from the salmagundis and dropped a little into his open mouth.

Her assistant was removing the roast pig from the Aga. "It's all ready," she said, "and I've put the beef into the hot cupboard. Do you want me to stay any longer?"

"Thanks, Frances, but I can manage now, there are two of the centre's staff coming in to help with the clearing up. I'll see you tomorrow."

The other girl took off her overall, smiled a good-night and left the kitchen. Darina filled the dog's bowl with water and put it by the table, then she found a tin opener and handed it to his master, who used it with the ease of long practice. As the lid came off, he looked up. "I'm sorry, I should have introduced myself; Gray Wyndham." He held out a hand. Darina hastily finished washing hers and shook it, liking the way she had to look up slightly into his eyes, almost the same colour as his dog's. "And you must be Darina Lisle, Nicholas said you were the cook in residence for the weekend."

He looked round the kitchen, taking in the roast pig which Darina had started to garnish with carrots and young turnips, the huge joint of beef visible through the glass doors of the hot cupboard and the array of Quaking Puddings waiting in their water bath. "Have you been responsible for all this food and," he gave a wave of the dog-food tin towards the refectory, "the astonishing display being filmed in there?"

"Frances helped." Darina looked at Gray. He seemed to be having difficulty getting the food out of the tin. He was frowning, his shoulders ridiculously tense with the effort of forcing the meat out into the dish. It came with a rush, and he added mixer biscuits and gave it to Bracken, who fell upon the food as though it was the first he had seen for several days. Gray straightened his lean frame, looked round for somewhere to throw the empty tin, found a fliptop bin, then had to remove its top in order to stuff the tin into the tightly packed contents. He stood looking at the debris—the vegetable peelings, pastry trimmings and poultry bones—his face working with emotion. Then he burst out, "It's revolting!"

Darina flushed. "I'm sorry," she said defensively, wiping down an immaculately clean surface, "we haven't had time to empty it."

Gray jammed the top of the bin back angrily. "Not that! All this," he waved his hand around the room again, "this *food!*" He made it sound the most disgusting of four-letter words. "I've never seen such obscene excess. Just how many gluttons have enrolled for this weekend?"

"Forty." The number was engraved on Darina's cooking heart.

"Forty!" Gray closed his eyes in an extremity of anguish. "You've got enough food here to feed forty times that number!"

Darina protested at the exaggeration but Gray was in full flight now.

"Do you know how much food it takes to keep an Ethiopian alive? What a Bangladeshi needs to keep going? What a down-and-out in London exists on?"

Darina's hands were still now as she looked at him in astonishment. "Why on earth did you come?" she asked.

The question jolted Gray out of his eloquence. He jammed his hands into his pockets (to prevent him strangling her? wondered Darina), leant back against the sink and looked at his shoes for a long minute. The emotion leaked out of him, the shoulders sagged, and when he looked up again the brown eyes were tired and drained. "I'm a writer," he said, then paused, as though further explanation was too much effort.

Darina searched her memory. "I'm afraid I don't think I've read any of your books," she said stiffly.

"It would surprise me if you had," said the man bitterly. "Apart from the first, my biographies hardly dented either the public or the academic consciousness." He studied his shoes for a moment longer. When he looked up again, his manner had changed, a diffident pride peeking out from behind the beard; like a schoolboy who has caught a frog but is not sure others will applaud his achievement. "I'm into something slightly different now, an historical novel—I think the term is blockbuster. It's set in the late seventeenth century. That's my period, but there are areas I need to gen up on, dress and food particularly. I ran into Nicholas at the Cambridge University Library and he suggested this weekend could help with the gastronomic side. I was at his college when I read history," he added as though that explained everything.

"And you didn't realise you'd actually have to eat as well?" Darina asked tartly.

"I never thought about it!" His gaze fell downwards again and a new thought struck him, equally horrific in its implications. "My God, don't tell me they all dress for dinner?"

She looked at his ancient jacket, well-worn trousers and checked Viyella shirt. "Well, it's not black tie but most people put on a suit."

He brightened slightly. "That I did bring. Though I've half a mind to come down like this. The whole thing needs putting into proportion." He bent and picked up the bowl, licked clean by the dog, grabbed the bag of biscuits and called to Bracken, who reluctantly left an entrancing smell hidden behind a cupboard and allowed himself to be led out. But as the man reached the door, he turned. "And you shouldn't allow dogs in the kitchen!"

For a moment Darina thought he must be joking, but he vanished without a glimmer of a smile and she was left staring at the door.

FOUR

Two hours later, Darina surveyed the refectory scene with satisfaction. The meal had been a success. Food had vanished with unbelievable swiftness and, in between ferrying in more Steak and Kidney pudding and casserole and dishing up wine sauce for Quaking Puddings, she had fielded innumerable queries on sources, recipes, methods and ingredients.

Now satiated eaters were sitting at the two long tables, relaxed and happy, lingering over Stilton and port. Even the TV crew seemed to have finished filming, though their strong lights still flooded the room, spotlighting every detail.

At the head of one table was Digby, his linen jacket exchanged for one of velvet, his wrinkled face mellow and distinguished over a bright green bow-tie. Beside him sat an insubstantially beautiful figure, the actress wife of a prominent food journalist. Her vivid blue eyes were watching Digby prepare her an apple.

The peel slithered over his long fingers, coiling neatly on his plate. He put down the naked fruit, held it upright, cut it into quarters, then carved out the core from each piece. Picking up a segment he raised it towards his companion, his eyes gazing into hers.

The rosy lips parted, a moist pink tongue curled daintily out from the tiny white teeth and Digby inserted the fruit into the soft mouth. The blue eyes like scraps of cornflower laughed back at him and the white teeth bit sharply through the crisp morsel, just missing the tips of his fingers. The two of them were oblivious of anyone else in the crowded room, fascinated by their effect on each other, as uninhibited as if they were on a desert island.

But there were at least two other pairs of eyes equally fascinated by the little scene.

Linda was sitting next to Nicholas, who headed the other long table. The producer showed no sign of fatigue from her efforts directing the cameras and was as fresh as when she had arrived, her black hair shining blue in the blaze of the TV lights. In front of her was a plate prettily set out with the few vegetable offerings the table had afforded. From time to time she delicately forked a fragment into her scarlet mouth. Darina had offered to produce an omelette but Linda had refused with lavish thanks that somehow managed to suggest even starvation would not bring her to consume anything produced by such an adept at carnivorous cooking. Nicholas was chatting happily, seemingly unaware that her gaze was fixed on Digby with a look of longing so open and vulnerable Darina had to look away, only to find her attention caught by someone else gazing at Digby and the beauty with equal intensity.

Still very attractive, once she must have been stunning. Now with middle age the paper-fine skin, powdered with freckles, had lost its tone, and wrinkles ate into the neck and around the eyes. What had once been fragility now verged on gauntness. But time had not dulled the cloud of red hair; vibrant as fire, it curled with artless charm round her classically boned features. She looked at Digby with disgust, jealousy and what Darina recognised with a jolt of uneasiness as pure hate.

Unwillingly, her eyes were drawn again to the object of so much emotion and found a third figure had joined the duo. Leaning over the actress was her husband, whispering something into her ear. She leant towards Digby, her hand caressing the soft velvet of his jacket, said a few words to him, then rose and followed her husband to the opposite end of the table, where he introduced her to the editor of a specialist foodie magazine. As they sat at the table, Darina saw the actress glance back towards Digby, giving him a little moue of apology.

Digby was looking back at her with speculation in his face. Darina knew that look—it meant the *bon viveur* had sighted a new delicacy. Well, it should mean she needn't have to worry about his advances for a little; this particular chase would require considerable ingenuity.

Carefully wiping such thoughts from her mind, Darina looked around at the other diners. Miss Makepeace was writing in a small book by her plate. She had carefully worked her way through every dish, addressing penetrating questions to the cook from time to time, particularly on the Yorkshire Christmas pie. She was the only one who had asked if the birds had been cooked at all before being baked and Darina had a nasty suspicion she was in for a thorough grilling at some stage. Miss Makepeace took food very seriously.

All around her were faces Darina recognised from the previous year, distinguished food writers, academics from many disciplines and simple food enthusiasts, all happily debating points on the various dishes or merely gossiping.

At the bottom of Nicholas's table was Gray Wyndham, now looking relaxed and almost happy. He seemed to have forgotten his distaste for such lavish provisioning. Darina had noticed no reluctance to consume several slices of Yorkshire pie and of roast beef, not to mention Quaking Pudding and a Buttered Orange. As he smiled at something his neighbour said, attractive crinkles appearing round his eyes, Darina thought she recognised his dining companion. She went to join them.

Gray rose from his seat. "Come and take the weight off your feet, you haven't sat down all evening. I apologise for my outburst earlier, I wouldn't have missed a morsel, it's all magnificent."

Darina sank down beside him with a sigh of relief.

"This is Charles Childe," Gray continued. "I think he wants to pick your brains for his restaurant."

"I thought I recognised you. Didn't you do that *Anything I Can Do* television series?"

Charles Childe visibly blew up to a larger size and his eyes sparkled. His slight frame was now clothed in a maroon silk suit of startling cut, a large and floppy striped bow-tie erupting from the collar of a tussore silk shirt. "Did you watch it?" He had the pleased air of a child praised for some precocious skill. "It was such fun. And, you know, it was all kosher, we didn't fake a thing, or practise beforehand."

Darina turned to Gray. "You didn't see any of the programmes?" He shook his head. "It was such a nice idea. Charles was the archetypal bachelor non-cook who took a different recipe each week and cooked it from scratch with a running commentary on what he didn't know, his doubts and difficulties. Every now and then Digby would chip in with advice and at the end he would comment on the finished result and identify the various techniques involved."

Charles's face darkened for a moment. "He would be a bit hard on me at times, I thought; after all, I *was* an amateur."

"The point of the programmes," Darina continued to Gray, "was that anything Charles Childe could do, the audience could manage, perhaps better after the benefit of Digby's advice." She turned to Charles. "You were awfully good, especially as the second series progressed. I should think it finally ended because you couldn't be classed as an amateur cook any longer."

Charles beamed. "That's what the TV people said. And I felt myself that I was really giving Digby a run for his money with the final few programmes. Actually," he leant towards Darina confidentially, "don't tell anyone, but when we did the second series, I took lessons from a cordon bleu cook on the side."

"Yet you were so clever at being the inexperienced cook."

"Well, I was an actor, after all. I could keep up the impression of doubts and mistakes and commit the odd amusing error without making a complete fool of myself in front of Digby. Some of those last recipes were quite complicated—all his, of course."

"And now you've got a restaurant. Where is it?"

Charles Childe needed no encouragement to tell Darina all about his venture in Wandsworth, "Which is *the* coming area. Lots of media people, some of them are becoming quite devoted clients. I was saying to Gray I think some old English recipes, updated of course, could make a great impression. That bird pie could be a sensation for lunches."

"Served with a salmagundi, of course," said Gray.

"My," exclaimed Darina, amusement shining in her eyes, "you're really catching on to the terminology."

"It's not difficult when it all tastes so delicious." His brown eyes twinkled back at her and she wondered where the contentious man from the kitchen had gone.

Charles Childe rose. "I must try and catch a few minutes with Linda. I'm sure we could work out a new food programme idea together." But he sat down again, his face crumpling in disappointment. "It looks as though I shall have to wait until later."

Darina and Gray looked towards the end of their table. The place beside Nicholas was empty and he was staring across the room. Linda had sat herself beside Digby in the seat vacated by the actress. The producer was leaning towards the chairman, talking quietly, her intense blue eyes fixed on his face. Digby was looking down at his plate, his attention on the nut he had just cracked, his fingers impatiently picking out fragments of flesh from the shattered shell.

Darina looked again at Nicholas and found him wearing a look of naked anger so intense it was as shocking as if she had opened a poison-pen letter. For the second time that evening she felt a voyeur. She looked away and met Gray's eyes.

"Not a pleasant chap, our Digby," he said quietly.

What an extraordinary comment, she thought. There had been nothing in the little scene to suggest Digby had in any way drawn the producer from Nicholas's side. To her surprise, she found herself opening her mouth to defend her cousin but before she could speak a delightful Irish voice said, "Now here's a great cook and I'd like to introduce myself."

Darina turned. Behind her was the red-haired woman who had been staring at Digby with such a complex mix of emotions. Not a trace of them remained. Open and friendly, the face was full of charm and a hand was being held out. "Rita Moore," said its owner, "and you're Darina Lisle?"

Darina took the hand and smiled back in delight. "How lovely to meet you. I have to tell you that your cookery book was one of the first I used and it is still one of my favourites."

"Ah, now that's going back some years, I thought it had been consigned to oblivion."

"Are you writing any new ones? I'd love to have another, your recipes are so useful, not complicated but a little different."

"Now, that's music to my ears, and I don't understand why a publisher doesn't hear the same tune. In fact, that's one reason I wanted to meet you: it's the historical side of cooking I'm working on now and I wondered if you'd be willing to tell me your sources and how you adapted the recipes."

"Come and join us." Darina edged towards Gray and made room for the cookery writer on the bench beside her. "I'd be delighted to help, but I'm afraid I'm no expert. I've just read some of the early cookery books and played around with a few of the recipes. Digby would be much more help to you."

Rita Moore looked rueful. "Sure and the great man and I fell out some time ago, an approach from me would be as welcome as poisonous mushrooms to a starving man."

Darina had to lean back as a hand shot past her towards the Irish woman and Gray Wyndham introduced himself saying, "Anyone disliked by Digby Cary has to be a friend of mine. I'm delighted to meet you, Miss Moore, or is it Mrs.?"

"Mr. Moore vanished some years ago, these days I'm Ms. But call me Rita. So it's a fact you're no friend of Digby's either?" She looked at him curiously.

"No, and had I known he was involved with this weekend, I should never have come."

Charles Childe clapped his hands together with a little cry of excitement, saying, "And I thought everyone *adored* the great man. Well! Perhaps we should start an 'I hate Digby Cary Society'; not that I do," he added hastily, "not really. Unless he gives my restaurant a really naughty review; then I shall kill him."

They all laughed and Gray said, "I'll lend you my shotgun."

Rita added, "And I'll find a poison, a toxin as undetectable as dew after the first flash of morning sun."

Darina said, "I should think Nicholas could contribute a blunt instrument."

"I am sure you mean no harm by it, but such talk is an offence against the Lord."

Comfortably broad vowels removed the sting from the rebuke. Darina turned to see a slightly flushed Miss Makepeace standing behind them, clasping her notebook to her chest. Awkward silence replaced the laughter, then Darina pulled herself together. "Will you join us, Miss Makepeace? You're right, one shouldn't joke about such things. How did you enjoy the meal?"

With a little more shifting, room was found for the older woman. She settled herself between Rita and Darina. "Very much," she said simply. "You have a real gift for cooking, Miss Lisle, and you've served us so many interesting dishes. I did wonder, though, why the emphasis on Christmas food?"

"Is there?" asked Darina in surprise. "I know there are mince-pies but only because I thought it would be nice to serve them as they used to be, with real meat as well as the dried fruit. Oh, of course, there's the Yorkshire Christmas pie, but surely that was served at other times as well?"

"You also have a boar's head. That was associated very strongly with Christmas until quite recently."

"Recently?" asked Rita with a slight smile.

"Oh yes, it only went out when the Commonwealth banned the Christmas celebrations in the seventeenth century." She looked at their gently amused faces. "Most Christmas food goes back to pre-Roman times. It's not a Christian festival at all, you know, it's the celebration of the old powers."

"The old powers?" Darina's question was gentle; Miss Makepeace was so very serious.

"Only the Church shields us from them," she said simply.

The silence that followed was broken by Digby rising and announcing that coffee would be served in the lounge. Darina rose with an apology and headed for the kitchen.

FIVE

With coffee safely served, Darina returned to the clearing up of the feast. Already the kitchen helpers had dealt with a quantity of washing up. Picking up a tray of clean silver, she carried it into the refectory and started returning knives and forks to the cutlery canteen concealed behind the serving screen. Her hands moved automatically and her mind drifted, becoming aware of just how exhausted she was. She wondered how much longer the redundant clearing up would take.

The click of the heavy oak door from the hall brought her back to matters in hand. Peering through the pierced wood of the screen, Darina saw Digby come in. Somehow she didn't think she could cope with Digby at this moment. She remained hidden behind the screen, wishing there was a way she could escape to the kitchen unseen, and watched him approach the long table, still scattered with remnants of the feast. He glanced around the room then picked up a spoon and attacked a Buttered Orange, swiftly demolished it and passed on to a syllabub. Darina felt shocked. After all those strictures on the evil of sweet things, to behave like a schoolboy raiding the larder at midnight. Somehow she had not expected such behaviour from Digby.

"Mr. Cary." It was the soft voice of Deborah Makepeace.

Digby hurriedly picked up a discarded napkin and held it over the half-eaten syllabub with a careless air. But Miss Makepeace, closing the refectory door, the large hide bag held firmly under one arm, a flush on her rounded cheeks, hadn't noticed his activity. She had other things on her mind.

"Mr. Cary," she repeated firmly, coming towards him, "at last I have managed to find you on your own. I think you owe me some explanation." She stood with quiet dignity in front of him.

"Explanation, dear lady?" Digby's voice had a nice note of amused enquiry but being so nearly caught out in his surreptitious guzzling had obviously upset him, for Darina could hear discomfort there as well. Serve him right to have to deal with a series of learned queries from Miss Makepeace.

"I have just read *The Case for Pastry.*" Miss Makepeace brought out a copy from her bag and held it towards Digby.

He stretched his hand towards her. "Let me sign it for you," he offered.

The book was hastily replaced in the hide bag. "Mr. Cary, you know what I am talking about. That is *my* book."

"*Your* book, what do you mean?" Amused condescension filled Digby's voice.

Darina was suddenly aware she was an eavesdropper. She took a step towards the edge of the screen but before she could turn the corner, Miss Makepeace spoke again, deep anger infusing her usually gentle voice. "*My* book, Mr. Cary. The book you were so interested in when we spoke at the end of last year's weekend. You remember asking to see it? And that I sent it to you so you could advise on my research? I never heard any more from you and now I read this"— she reached back in her bag, retrieved the book and read from its cover—"this *History of Pastry and Its Uses in England from Mediaeval to Modern Times.*" She paused for a moment, the brown eyes magnified by the thick lenses looking at the big man steadily, unwaveringly. "It is my work, Mr. Cary, all my work. Oh, you've reworded it, it's now written in your style, very different from the plain way I set it out, and there are some additional recipes, all of which you have published before"—scorn filled her voice—"but otherwise it is my book."

For a moment there was complete silence in the room. Beyond Digby's rigid back, Darina could see Deborah Makepeace, feet planted firmly on the polished wood floor, shoulders squared, a yeoman soldier determined to stand his ground even though the odds were overwhelming.

"I saw it in my local bookshop"—the quiet voice was gaining strength and depth—"and bought it out of interest, wondering how your research would compare with mine. And then I read it. Fact after fact taken from my manuscript. I looked to see if you had acknowledged my work but the only acknowledgement in the whole book is to your editor. Then I thought you would have a word of explanation for me when we met here, but you might have been avoiding me it has been so difficult to approach you."

"Miss Makepeace"—Digby broke in on her, his voice urbane but edged with menace—"you are suffering some form of delusion. The book is entirely my own work. You may well have been undertaking similar research . . ." His tone lightened, the napkin was released and he put his hand on her shoulder. "I know what a busy little bee you are." He gave an indulgent laugh, celebrated writer condescending to ambitious amateur. Miss Makepeace stiffened and stepped back. Digby's hand dropped to his side as he continued, "It may even be our research followed similar lines. As I never received your book" —there was a flash of light from Miss Makepeace's glasses as her head jerked—"I don't know. But there is no question *at all*"—the words shot out with the force of bullets—"of my ever making use of someone else's research."

Deborah Makepeace looked at him, incredulity written large in every line of her kindly face.

"Furthermore"—the menace was back in Digby's voice—"if you repeat these accusations in public, I shall be compelled to sue you for slander."

There was the hiss of breath sharply taken in. Deborah Makepeace seemed to grow taller; no longer was she an unassuming country woman, some inner power had taken over and she faced Digby Cary as an equal. Even the country accent added strength, a roots-deep belief in the rightness of her cause. "You know you had my only copy, you told me it would be safe with you. And as I wrote the book, I destroyed my notes. Those notes took me fifteen years . . . fifteen years of research fitted into a life of harder work than you could ever understand.

"And who would believe my word against yours? Oh, you are confident and no doubt you feel you have every right to be. Well, there are powers beyond either of us, Mr. Cary. I will leave it to them to bring justice and, believe me, justice will be done."

There was a Messianic ring to her voice and Digby dropped back a pace, raised his hand as though to ward off some danger, then thrust it deep into his jacket pocket. "We have nothing more to say to one another," he stated and walked swiftly from the room.

As the door shut behind him, the strength seemed to drain out of Miss Makepeace, who sagged and clutched at the table. Heedless of the consequences, Darina dropped the knives she had been holding, and came into the refectory. But before she could say anything, Miss Makepeace rushed from the room.

Darina stood looking at the table and its load of plundered dishes but all she could see was Digby's back gradually stiffening as Deborah Makepeace flung her accusations at him, and the convulsive scrunching of the linen napkin he had used to cover his illicit sweet.

Surely the accusation couldn't be true? Surely Digby would not lift someone else's work without acknowledgement? However lax his sexual morals, she had always believed her cousin's professional integrity to be unassailable. No, Miss Makepeace must have been mistaken.

After all, there could not be that many sources for researching pastry, and two people working in the same field would be bound to duplicate many pieces of information. Then Darina remembered the brief look she had taken at the book, the complex detail it seemed to offer. Could Digby possibly have had time for such painstaking research? Perhaps he had used an assistant. Yet surely he would have told her if that had been the case? Was he ashamed of having to hire help in a field he had made so peculiarly his own?

Unbidden, the picture of Digby furtively scoffing the sweets he had affected to despise slipped into Darina's mind. With a small shiver, she turned from these new insights into her cousin's character; she had neither time nor energy to grapple with this sort of problem. Feeding the symposiasts was enough for her to cope with. There was still a tart to make for tomorrow, not to mention the rest of the clearing up to supervise. She flung back the long hair that had worked its way over her shoulder, picked up the boar's head and took it through to the kitchen.

SIX

It was about midnight that the commotion broke out. Darina had at last managed to get to bed. She was just putting out the light when furious barking and the sound of someone's terrified shouting came clearly through her bedroom door. She waited for a moment, then, when the noise seemed to increase rather than diminish, slipped out of bed, drew her dressing gown around her and opened the door.

Her room was on the second floor at the head of the staircase, and the noise was coming straight up from the hall. Leaning over the balustrade, Darina got a confused impression of a dog savaging one or maybe two men. She dashed back into her room, snatched up the full kettle of water and ran down the stairs, reaching the bottom just as a snarling and maddened Bracken was dragged off an hysterical Charles Childe by his master. Blood was flowing copiously from Charles's hand and he was incoherent, sobbing with terror and pain.

Gray Wyndham had his hand through the dog's collar, twisting it so that the animal was almost choking. Bracken was still impotently trying to get at his victim, lurching forward against the restricting grasp. Gray greeted Darina's arrival with relief. "Thank God! Can you look after Charles whilst I put this wretched hound away?"

By now the choking effect of the twisted collar had done its work: Bracken had ceased to struggle and stood trembling violently, trying to gulp in air. He put up no resistance to being led away through the refectory.

Darina put down the redundant kettle and turned towards Charles. He had sunk on to the bottom two steps of the staircase, holding his damaged hand and moaning quietly, swaying backwards and forwards. Blood was pouring down his wrist, over the maroon jacket and on to the polished wood of the stairs. Darina felt in the pocket of her dressing gown and found a couple of paper handkerchiefs. She pressed them against the damaged hand, where they instantly became sodden. "Try this," said a voice and an enormous linen handkerchief appeared over her shoulder. Gratefully Darina wound it tightly round Charles's hand. Though the pristine white rapidly darkened, blood ceased to drip.

"What on earth has been happening?" asked Nicholas.

"My God," said another voice, "is he all right?"

Darina kept tight hold of the wrapped hand and looked up. Rita Moore was coming down the staircase.

She wore an amazing red dressing gown wreathed in a golden dragon, the colours making a wild symphony with her hair, her feet thrust into heelless slippers of the same red.

Nicholas had exchanged his jacket for a camel cardigan and had a biro in his hand. Having produced his handkerchief, he seemed at the limit of his resourcefulness and stood looking at the bloody scene, his face growing paler by the second.

Rita was more practical. "The poor man! Bring him up to my room, we'll see just how bad that hand is."

Darina bent down and, slipping an arm round Charles, pulled him to his feet. His face was sheet-white and for a moment she feared he was going to pass out. Nicholas came to his other side and between them they managed to get him up the stairs to Rita's room, just off the landing. Quite small, it still had room for a comfortable armchair and a writing table as well as a dressing table and a bed furnished with a crewelwork cover. It also had its own bathroom. They sat Charles on the side of the bath and Rita turned on the cold tap in the basin. Then she took the damaged hand, unwound the handkerchief, removed the sodden tissues and placed the now sluggishly bleeding wound under the running water.

With the blood washed away, they could see where the dog had sunk his teeth deeply into the side of the hand, tearing into the flesh. "I'm afraid that's going to need stitches," Rita said.

Charles moaned. He had held his head away from the hand, refusing to look at the wound. He still hadn't uttered a word. Most of the time he kept his eyes closed, the impossibly long lashes resting on bloodless cheeks.

Rita rewrapped Nicholas's handkerchief round the hand, then eased Charles up from the bath and led him back into the bedroom.

"It's brandy that will help you now," she said and placed him in the armchair. She picked up an open bottle from the table. "Will you get me that glass from the bathroom, dear?" she asked Darina, who saw the one on the table still held a fingerful of liquid.

Darina brought the glass; Rita poured in a good slug and held it to Charles's lips. Deathly pale, he had the bedraggled look of a refugee, with his ruined jacket hanging loose and open and smudges of blood on his cream shirt. He took a deep draught of the liquid and sighed.

Gray came into the room, breathing rapidly as though he had run up the stairs. "I can't tell you how much I regret what has happened. I had no idea people would still be up or I would have had Bracken on a lead. What were you coming downstairs for at that time of night anyway?" The aggression of guilt infected his voice, making the enquiry harsh and accusing.

Charles closed his eyes for a moment, then opened them and looked at Gray. "I suddenly remembered I hadn't a copy of the programme. I thought I'd like to look at one before going to bed, prepare myself for tomorrow."

"Now I feel responsible," broke in Nicholas, his broad brow furrowed with distress. "If I'd remembered to give you copies when you arrived this need not have happened."

Charles's uninjured hand came up and took the glass of brandy so he could finish it.

"He's going to need hospital treatment," said Rita, looking directly at Gray.

"Where's the nearest casualty department?" he asked, turning to Nicholas, who shrugged his shoulders helplessly.

"Yeovil, I should think," offered Darina, aware she was the nearest to being a local. "It must be closer than Bristol. Turn right at the end of the drive, left when you meet the main road and then follow the signs. The hospital's well signposted once you reach the town."

"I'll get the car round to the front of the house, perhaps you could help him downstairs."

Ten minutes later, Darina, Nicholas and Rita watched the car pull away down the drive, Charles leaning weakly against the neck rest of the passenger seat.

"Well," said Rita, "we'd better try and get some sleep before the night's quite over. At least we don't seem to have woken everyone up, though how Linda and Digby can have slept through that racket is more than a body can comprehend, Charles made enough noise to wake the dead. Lord, now where's he going?"

Nicholas was charging up the stairs, grim purpose stiffening his body. He reached the landing and turned left, grasping the doorknob of the bedroom next to Rita's. He stood holding it for a moment then pushed the door quietly open. He listened, then turned on the light. "He's not there," he said hollowly.

Darina had picked up her kettle and followed Rita up to stand behind him. She looked over Nicholas's shoulder. The room was immaculate, apart from a half-unpacked suitcase lying on the bed. There was no sign of any occupant. Nicholas switched off the light and closed the door. He turned and looked down the corridor the other side of the landing, towards the last door. The others followed his gaze, then Rita laid her hand on his arm. "The man's probably still working, Nicholas; his pyjamas were in the case!"

Nicholas brightened for a moment, then grew despondent again. "That needn't mean a thing."

"Shall I check?" suggested Darina.

Nicholas shook his head miserably. "I think not, we should all get to bed." He turned to his own room. Rita and Darina looked after him for a moment, exchanged glances then said good-night.

SEVEN

Darina climbed the polished stairs to the second floor, every bone in her body aching with weariness. Stamina was one of her great assets as a cook—people seldom realised the enormous physical effort that went into a day's concentrated cooking—but there were times when she wondered if she had had enough. Where was she going in her profession? Her mind went back to a scene with Digby after the clearing up had been finished.

She had needed nutmeg for a tart she was preparing for the following day's lunch. Her special little grater contained only a tiny piece, the food of our ancestors is heavy on nutmeg, and the kitchen yielded only ready ground. But Darina remembered the spice box in the housekeeper's room.

As she was opening the little lids of the round box—revealing in turn pale cardamom pods, tightly rolled cinnamon sticks, enamel-bright chilli peppers and rough brown allspice berries in her search for the small, egg-shaped nutmeg—the door opened, a hand fell heavily on her shoulder and a wine-laden breath murmured in her ear, "Ah, my little cousin!"

Jumping with shock, Darina dropped the spice box, which scattered its treasures across the floor.

"Digby!" she exclaimed crossly.

"Startled you, did I?" he asked. He made no attempt to help her pick up the spices but sat down heavily in front of his typewriter, turned sideways on and watched her kneel on the floor to scoop up and sort out handfuls of pods and beans, placing each in its separate little section of the box. There was silence for a moment as she worked, then he asked, "Does ambition eat at you, Darina?"

She looked up at him but met such turbulence in the eyes that usually held nothing more than shallow sparkle that she immediately looked down again. It had been a glimpse into a private hell. Shaken, she could think of nothing to say.

"Aren't you interested in making a career for yourself?" The voice was rough and insistent.

Carefully Darina allowed allspice berries to trickle into the box. "Yes, I'd like to succeed," she said at last.

"Ah, but what at? Do you just want to be that nice Darina Lisle, *such* a good cook, my dear, and clears up as well?" His imitation of the Mayfair hostesses who passed on her name was wickedly accurate. "Or are you aiming higher, at establishing yourself as a force in the world of food?"

Keeping a nutmeg in her hand, Darina put the spice box back on the dresser then leant against the pale green wood, her mind caught by what he was asking. "What I'd really like is to have a hotel, somewhere I can provide a marvellous atmosphere, superb food and lovely rooms, where people could come and stay and get away from ordinary, everyday cares." For a moment she forgot the stresses of the weekend and lost herself in the dream.

Digby looked at her with envy. "Ah, Darina, my dear, you're a creator. I'm just a commentator, someone who preys on other people's work."

Darina looked at him sharply.

"You're right to have nothing to do with me, I'm worthless. If only you'd been ten years older, if I'd realised what you were before I met Sarah, it might all have been so different. You could have kept me straight. Do you know what your father used to say to me? 'Digby, things come to you too easily. That facility could be your greatest curse.' And he was right, I've never worked hard enough at anything. I've grabbed at opportunities as they've come along, without a thought of where they were leading. Perhaps if your father had lived, he'd have made me think more deeply."

"Would you have listened?" Darina was getting tired of his self-pity.

Digby gave a harsh little laugh. "You're right, of course. I was already too big for my boots before he died. But an anchor disappeared when he went. Those visits to your home meant so much to me. I remember you as a long-legged streak of a girl, fair hair in plaits, with a wonderful smile. You made me feel I could conquer the world. You never smile at me like that now." He paused for a moment, looking down at his hands, loosely linked together. "And how you loved messing around in the kitchen, your food was surprisingly good, and you would be so pleased when everything got eaten." He fell silent, the fingers of his big hands locking and unlocking.

"Mother and I were still there," said Darina tartly. "Why didn't you visit us?"

He looked up, the eyes wary now. "It wasn't the same and I was very busy." His eyes fell before Darina's straightforward gaze. Then he flashed her the most charming of his smiles. "So, my dear, what about your hotel, what are your plans?"

Darina laughed, "It's only a dream, Digby. Starting hotels requires money and I can't see how I can ever amass enough. Even if I could find someone to lend me capital, I doubt the sort of place I have in mind could produce sufficient to service the debt and provide a reasonable cash flow. No, I just hope to build up a business cooking for others, perhaps eventually create an outside catering company . . . which reminds me, I must get back to my tart, I only came in here to find a nutmeg."

Digby swung round to his typewriter. "And I must get down to my talk for tomorrow. Could you tell Nicholas that I'm here? I think he's in the bar—he was trying to get hold of me earlier for some reason and I'd better attempt to sort out whatever little bee he has in his bonnet now."

Darina returned to the kitchen feeling, despite everything that had transpired earlier that evening, more in charity with Digby than for many years. A human being had reappeared from behind the glittering façade.

When the tart had been placed in the oven, she sought out Nicholas. As she came into the hall, there was a surge of symposiasts emerging from the bar and disappearing through a side door to the annexe. The party seemed to be breaking up. In the bar she found Nicholas talking with Linda. Rita Moore was chatting with Gray and Charles sat in a deep chair listening to them, leaning forward, ready to break in whenever the opportunity arose. Miss Makepeace had a large book on her lap but her eyes were staring vacantly into the empty fireplace. Everywhere were ashtrays bearing stubbed cigarettes, glasses more or less empty, the look of a good party just ended. And here was the home team, enjoying its aftermath before going to bed themselves. How strange that that little journey across from the main building to the annexe should divide the group so precisely.

Nicholas looked up and Darina, apologising for the interruption, gave Digby's message, but he hardly seemed to take it in, merely nodding absently before returning to his conversation with Linda.

"You still working?" asked Gray, who had broken off whatever he was saying to Rita as Darina entered the bar.

"Not much more to do now. Anything I can get anyone?" No one took up the offer and she returned to the kitchen to finish a few last jobs before removing her tart from the oven and making her way upstairs to the second floor. She deliberately did not say good-night to Digby.

How strange physical attraction was, she thought now, as sleep proved elusive for her tired mind. There was Digby who seemed able to attract any female. Any female but herself—was that why she had such a strange attraction for him? The lure of the unattainable? And there was poor Nicholas, desperate to hold the interest of Linda, who seemed prepared to give him her time until the moment Digby should appear. Who appeared far from interested in her.

Darina thought about Linda for a moment. The producer could never be her favourite sort of person but she had an odd sort of charm and her face was undoubtedly fascinating. Were she a man though, Darina decided that she would prefer the open and warm Rita, despite her extra years. And Gray seemed to be getting on with her remarkably well. For a moment Darina regretted that her duties prevented her from spending more time with the symposiasts. It had been a long while since she had met a man who interested her as much as Gray, even stirred her. Not since Jack.

She felt the sharp twist of some vital part that came every time she remembered Jack. Witty Jack, devil-may-care Jack, who took her young heart and played on it like a jazz virtuoso. Jack who made her laugh and love and tried to teach her to treat life with his own lightness.

"Think of the way you handle pastry," he'd said one morning as they lay arguing in bed, he trying to persuade her to give up a buffet she had arranged to do for an old client because he wanted her to go to Paris with him, she attempting to make him consider life more seriously. "Your hands hardly seem to touch the flour and fat yet it achieves shape and then rises effortlessly. That's the way to deal with everything else." Then before she could protest, he had reached for her. "And pastry's not the only thing you make rise effortlessly, you long-legged witch."

She'd loved him, totally, wonderfully, passionately. And when he'd gone his witty, bawdy way to some other girl, she'd sworn men were not for her and picked up the none-too-secure threads of her small catering business, concentrating on establishing a reputation for reliability as well as good cooking.

Not that many opportunities for diversion had been offered after the Jack affair. Was it the embarrassment of her height? The impossibility of her working hours, or the fact she'd never learned that lightness of touch with men she could so easily use with pastry? Couldn't produce the light, flirtatious remarks that set a man at his ease, made him feel attractive and interesting. Gray Wyndham had seemed too intelligent to need that sort of approach. And if anyone lacked lightness of touch, it was tall, shaggy, prickly Gray.

But perhaps he would respond to a little subtle flattery. After all, hadn't Digby's advances, unwelcome though they might be, made her feel some of the glow that had filled her during that time with Jack? Made her feel feminine, alluring even. Perhaps flattery did get you everywhere. Her thoughts gradually becoming confused, Darina drifted off into an uneasy sleep.

EIGHT

The alarm clock went at 6:00 A.M. Darina cursed, her head full of cotton wool. The last thing she wanted was to leave the warm security of her bed. But half an hour later she was downstairs and entering the kitchen, neatly dressed in a white overall, her hair falling in a pale gold shower down her back.

The last remnants of sleep were banished as an ecstatic dog jumped all over her, no trace now of the vicious aggression of the previous night. Darina pushed him away, laughing at his exuberance. "Bracken, you shouldn't be in here, what would your master say? Didn't he shut you up properly?"

Then her eyes fell on a large quiche tin lying on the floor, its loose bottom several feet from its rim. "Oh, no," she groaned, "Bracken, you haven't! Oh, you wicked dog!" The tart she had left sitting on the kitchen table to cool the previous night was no more. The dog, fully aware of his iniquity, slunk under the table, then peeked his head out, imploring eyes begging forgiveness.

Despite her anger, Darina had to smile. "I suppose I can hardly blame you, I should have put it safely away."

A quick inspection showed her that a faulty latch on the far kitchen door meant a dog could easily push it open and that the boiler room door had obviously not been properly secured. Hardly surprising considering the stresses of the previous evening. Well, lunch would just have to do without the tart, there wasn't the time to make another. There should be ample without it but Darina mourned the loss of the prettily decorated top, the pastry cut in a pattern meant to resemble virginal keys. It had been copied from a seventeenth-century cookery book and she had hoped it would create quite a stir.

Pushing the thought behind her, Darina shut the dog securely in the boiler room and started on preparations for breakfast, cooking a huge kedgeree and laying out some pickled herring and sliced cold meat from the leftovers of dinner. She set out butter on the previously laid long tables in the refectory and dishes of quince preserve, the original "marmalade." Back in the kitchen, she looked around for the orange marmalade. A speciality of the Abbey Conference Centre housekeeper, Miss Dawkins had been most anxious it should be served to this army of discerning gastronomes. Where was it she said it was kept? Of course, the housekeeper's room.

Darina opened the door, switched on the light and was halfway across the room, making for the glass-fronted preserve cupboard, before she realised something was lying on the floor. A few seconds later she realised that that something was Digby.

For a moment Darina thought that he was asleep, that he had worked late and been overcome with tiredness. But there was something odd about his position. He lay, in shirt-sleeves and trousers, like a small child asleep on its stomach, right arm flung above his head, left leg drawn up. Like a small child but also in the classic position of a murder victim.

Murder was far from Darina's mind but she did not need to bend and touch Digby's shoulder to know that he was dead. But bend she did, touch she did, and immediately drew back with shock at the cold rigidity of the body.

She knelt back on her heels and looked at him. How had he died? Heart attack? Now that she could see his face, she noted that the eyes were wide open and staring, but staring with surprise, not pain. Death had called like an unexpected but not necessarily unwelcome visitor. No, it couldn't have been his heart. Gently, Darina reached forward and forced herself to pull the cold eyelids down over the blue eyes, their sparkle, either kindly or malevolent, lost forever.

Something about the position of his chest caught her attention. Straining against his weight, she tried to heave his shoulder up. Almost immediately she had to let the body sink back against the floor, but not before she had glimpsed the handle of a knife sticking out of where she assumed his heart could be.

It was then the shock hit her. Her stomach heaved, she clasped her hands to her mouth, closed her eyes and tried to make her mind a complete blank. Breathing deeply, she felt bile in her throat, tasted its sourness, then, with a hard swallow, returned it whence it came.

Rising unsteadily, averting her face from the figure on the floor, now no more Digby than was the chair or the door, Darina made her way to the kitchen. Clinging like some shipwrecked loon to doorknob, chair-back and table, she reached the sink, turned on the cold tap, splashed her face with the water and cupped her hands to drink its cool, cleansing freshness. Finally she stood with her face wet, breathing deeply but evenly. Gradually her mind began to work again. Her first thought: she must tell Nicholas.

It took a little time for the professor to open the door to her insistent knocking, the delay instantly explained by the towel wrapped clumsily round his bony frame and legs dripping water onto the carpet as he stood holding the door slightly ajar.

"I'm so sorry to drag you from your bath," Darina said quietly, "but I'm afraid there's been an accident."

"Accident? What accident?" Nicholas was testy.

"Digby's dead." Darina could think of no way to soften the news.

"Dead?" Nicholas stared at her for a moment, then his hand renewed its grip on his towel. "Come in, come in." He opened the door wide, ushering Darina inside. "Now, tell me what you mean."

Darina gave brief details of her discovery, Nicholas's face whitening as she spoke.

"Dreadful," he said when she had finished, "dreadful, it will ruin the symposium." Something told him a slightly different reaction was called for. "I mean, I can't believe it. Digby, dead!"

"Should we call a doctor or the police?" asked Darina, her heart sinking. She had come to Nicholas expecting him to take command, to remove the burden of decision-making from her shoulders.

"Police?" he repeated. "Is that necessary?"

"He has a knife sticking out of his chest," repeated Darina bleakly. "It could have been self-inflicted . . ." Her voice trailed away.

Nicholas gazed at her in awful fascination. "A knife?" Then he pulled himself together. "Digby take his own life? Nonsense, it's impossible."

"Then," said Darina slowly, "it has to be . . ." But she couldn't bring herself to say the word and Nicholas completed the proposition for her.

"Murder," he said, his voice extremely matter-of-fact. "Of course you are right, the police must be called." The academic was in command now. "You'd better ring them whilst I get some clothes on. Then wait in the kitchen and I'll come and look at, at . . ." he faltered a moment, then finished firmly, "look at Digby." He walked through to the bathroom and Darina went downstairs.

There was a telephone in the housekeeper's room but she couldn't bring herself to go in there again so she went to the public call-box in the short corridor between the hall and the bar.

As she came back into the hall, Nicholas descended the stairs, pulling a light sweater over slacks and open-necked shirt.

"A constable should be here quite soon," Darina said, "and the police say not to enter the room again until they get here."

Robbed of his purpose, Nicholas stood at the bottom of the stairs looking around aimlessly.

"Come and have a coffee in the kitchen," suggested Darina, leading the way. She lifted the lid of the Aga hot-plate, put on the kettle, then started grinding coffee beans. Nicholas, pacing up and down the kitchen, raised his head irritably at the noise.

"Do you have to do that? Sorry," he added as Darina looked at him in surprise, "I'm trying to realise Digby's dead. And to work out the implications." He continued pacing up and down, hands thrust into trouser pockets. Darina reached for the tin of instant coffee and spooned granules into mugs.

Nicholas took the steaming mug from her and sipped automatically, his mind still wrestling with the impossibility of the situation. "When did the police say they'd get here? God knows what we can do to rescue the symposium. I suppose they'll want to question everyone." He swung back along the path he was eroding into the kitchen floor. "If we set aside the morning for that, perhaps we could begin proceedings this afternoon."

Darina gazed at him in astonishment. A man he had known closely was dead, probably murdered by someone who had dined with them last night, and all Nicholas seemed able to think of was lectures and discussions on long-vanished food.

Nicholas paused in his pacing. "What made you suggest he could have taken his own life?"

"It was just something he said last night." Darina hesitated, finding it difficult to express her sense of Digby's despair, accidie. Had it just been her imagination, working on a trick of drunken sentimentality on top of her suspicions after overhearing the scene with Deborah Makepeace?

"Did you close the door of the housekeeper's room after you left just now?"

Darina thought for a moment then shook her head: Nicholas turned on his heel and darted out of the kitchen. She followed him reluctantly, some instinct telling her he should not be allowed near the scene alone.

He stood at the open door. The light was still on, competing with the grey dawning of a damp day edging itself reluctantly through the high window. Digby still lay on the floor, his luxuriant hair curling over the edge of his collar. Darina thought it had no right to look so springy and alive, then noticed with surprise the pale scalp shining through a thinning area on the crown of his head. How that must have upset him, she thought.

Nicholas was looking round the room, his feet carefully toeing an invisible line across the threshold of the door. "One can hardly tell anything from here," he said irritably, "but I should have thought stabbing oneself through the chest is an unlikely way to commit suicide; cutting the throat would surely be the natural course to take." He sounded as though such considerations were a daily routine with him. "I suppose the knife must have been one of those on the table."

Darina looked at the display, which appeared to be much as Digby had arranged it. Then she took a second look—was the boning knife missing? She remembered the feel of its razor sharpness and closed her eyes for a moment. She didn't want to be here, she wanted to wake up and find the whole nightmare was nothing more than that.

As they both continued to study the scene, a bell jangled melodiously and in the kitchen a clapper in a bank of bells swung above a neatly written label proclaiming "Front Door."

Nicholas and Darina went together to find two uniformed police waiting on the step, backed by a patrol car with a disembodied voice spilling out of an open window.

Officialdom took over.

NINE

Much later Inspector Grant watched his sergeant close the door behind Professor Turvey and said, "Well, Bill, what do you think we have here?"

Sergeant William Pigram flashed his superior a quick grin. "Four and twenty blackbirds baked in a pie, sir?" Then he collected himself, picked up his notebook and sat in the chair opposite the writing table that had been pressed into service as a desk.

They were in a smallish room on the other side of the hall from the refectory. Normally used as a quiet retreat for conference members or symposiasts, it was furnished with some deep leather chairs, a couple of writing tables equipped with upright chairs, a few low tables generously supplied with out-of-date magazines and two bookcases filled with dusty-looking books. Its window jutted out into the front garden, where a steady drizzle now stained the still-profuse roses. Grant had requisitioned it as suitable for an interview and incident room, ordering a telephone to be installed as quickly as possible. William thought its air of neglected gloom very apposite to the enquiry in hand.

"Take me through events so far, Bill," said his superior, leaning back against the uncomfortably straight-backed chair he had placed behind the table and lacing his hands behind his head. He fixed his gaze on a large engraving of the Monument with foxing round the edges.

William gave him a quick glance before he flicked over the pages of his notebook and paused to assemble the details they had heard in their proper order. Over the period he had been working with the inspector, he had learned that these summings-up provided an opportunity for the superior officer both to clarify his own impression of events and to check his junior's grasp of the situation in hand. It was always a taxing experience. He was expected to interweave details heard from several sources, straighten out confused accounts, identify conflicting statements and provide a smooth narrative. And Grant was a tiger for details, pouncing immediately on any misremembrance. It was worse than his viva voce at Oxford. But so far this situation seemed fairly straightforward.

William took another glance at his notebook and began.

"Deceased is Digby Cary, well-known food writer and television cook. With Professor Turvey, Head of Archaeology at St. Bernard's College, Cambridge, he founded the Society of Historical Gastronomes. This is their second annual symposium. Members arrived during yesterday afternoon and early evening, also a television team from the local network. Only the producer, Linda Stainmore, stayed the night. The rest left around 10:30 P.M. and returned again around 9:00 A.M. this morning. They are now filming anything they think might be useful to a programme on how the founding father of the society was murdered, without actually managing to get near the scene of the crime."

Grant shot his junior a cold look over the half frames of his spectacles and William forced himself to curb his errant story-telling instincts.

"By eleven o'clock last night, all outside staff had departed and the back door had been locked after them by the cook, Darina Lisle, who placed the key in its usual position on top of the lintel. Constable Clifton found it there this morning. The deceased was working in the housekeeper's room and Miss Lisle was asked by him to inform Professor Turvey of his location. She gave this message to the professor just after ten minutes past eleven. In the bar with him at the time were Miss Stainmore, Ms. Rita Moore, Miss Deborah Makepeace, Mr. Gray Wyndham and Mr. Charles Childe. Those members sleeping in the annexe had left the main building shortly before. Professor Turvey has stated he did not go to see the deceased but went up to his room to work on his symposium address. Apparently everyone else left the bar at about the same time, Mr. Wyndham to take his dog for a walk, the rest to go to bed.

"Miss Lisle returned to the kitchen. She stated she was not aware of anyone coming down to visit the housekeeper's room between then and 11:45 P.M., at which time she went to bed. However, there is a corridor from the stairs past the kitchen to the scene of the crime and it could have been possible for someone to visit Cary without her knowledge. The walls are thick and sound does not carry well there.

"At midnight, or thereabouts, Miss Lisle was preparing for sleep when she heard a noise in the hall. On investigation, she found the dog attacking Mr. Childe who claimed to have gone downstairs for a copy of the symposium programme (there is a pile of them on the table in the hall). The dog had just returned from his walk and was not on a leash. Mr. Wyndham gained control of the dog and shut him in the boiler room. This is opposite one of the doors to the kitchen and just along from the housekeeper's room.

"Mr. Childe was taken to Ms. Moore's bathroom to have his hand seen to. Mr. Wyndham then took him to Yeovil Hospital casualty department, where several stitches were inserted. The others went to bed after ascertaining that Mr. Cary was not in his room and had not been to bed that evening.

"Mr. Childe and Mr. Wyndham apparently stated to Professor Turvey that they returned to the abbey at approximately 3:30 A.M. There was no sign of anyone awake at that time. They locked the front door, turned off the light in the hall and went to bed in the room they are sharing." William firmly banished from his wayward mind a picture of the effete Childe and the shaggy Wyndham in their pyjamas sitting up in Elizabethan formality in adjoining twin beds. "Miss Lisle came down at around 6:30 A.M., found the dog in the kitchen, a faulty latch on the kitchen door and the boiler-room door ajar—she thinks it had not been properly shut. The dog had eaten a tart she had left on the kitchen table.

"Whilst preparing breakfast, she stated she entered the house-keeper's room at about 7:00 A.M. She found Digby Cary dead on the floor. She apparently closed his eyelids then tried to turn over his body, failed, but saw a knife was sticking out of his chest. She notified Professor Turvey, who instructed her to ring the police.

"Constables White and Clifton arrived at 8:05 A.M. They made the lower floor off limits to the symposiasts but allowed Miss Lisle to use the kitchen to provide breakfast in the refectory. Constable White remained in the kitchen with her.

"First downstairs were Mr. Wyndham at 8:10 A.M., who was refused permission to take his dog for a walk until reinforcements

arrived and he could be accompanied, then Miss Makepeace at 8:15
A.M. After that there was a veritable flood of hungry gastronomes
from both the abbey and the annexe. General reactions were shock
at the death and relief breakfast would be served. Most upset, according to Clifton, seemed to be Ms. Moore and Miss Stainmore.
Miss Stainmore was not allowed to telephone her station but made
contact with one of her television crew when they were refused
admission on their arrival at 9:00 A.M.

"We arrived at 8:45 A.M. After viewing the scene of the crime and
arranging for forensic examination and photography, we breakfasted
with some of the symposiasts until the doctor arrived to examine the
body at 9:25 A.M. He gave it as his opinion that death could have
occurred any time between 11:00 P.M. and 1:00 A.M. but was probably nearer 11:00 than 1:00. He stated death seemed to have occurred
as the result of a kitchen knife being driven under the third rib into
the heart. It would have been instantaneous. The absence of blood
was not considered unusual. There was a selection of brand-new
kitchen knives on the table in the centre of the housekeeper's room.
Miss Lisle thinks that the murder weapon could be a boning knife
that had been amongst them yesterday evening.

"The body has now been removed and a post mortem will be
carried out, probably this afternoon. The coroner has been informed
of the death.

"Preliminary statements have been taken from Miss Lisle and Professor Turvey. Forensics are now examining the scene of the crime.
All symposiasts are at present in the conference centre, their names
and addresses are being checked, and all are anxious to know what is
to happen to the symposium. Most anxious is Professor Turvey."
William finished his account in the same smooth, unemotional tones
he had used throughout. Grant shot him another cold look but the
younger man returned it unabashed.

Grant pushed his chair further away from the table, leant back to
balance it on its back legs, then placed both of his on the table in
front of him, revealing a pair of violently coloured argyle socks. He
returned his hands to their interlocked position behind his head and
began a study of the plastered ceiling. "What do you think, Bill?"

Grant was fond of asking his junior for his opinion. William hoped
it meant he considered it valuable but realised it was more likely his

powers of deduction were being tested. He thought for a moment. "The only symposiasts who knew Cary was working in the housekeeper's room were those in the bar when Miss Lisle gave the professor the message. We ought, therefore, to be able to discount the others."

Grant swivelled a chilly grey eye in his direction. "What about the window in the housekeeper's room? Could someone have seen Cary working there through that? The room's below ground level, remember, and there are no curtains."

William cursed himself for not thinking of that one. "It will have to be checked, sir. It's so high and narrow, though, I think it unlikely."

"Very well, continue."

"The dog was more or less on the loose, probably in a highly excited state after the attack on Charles Childe, so it would seem unlikely the murderer would have been able to enter the housekeeper's room without some commotion being raised after about 12:15 A.M."

"So," Grant mused reflectively, "death probably occurred between 11:00 P.M., when Miss Lisle last spoke to the deceased—assuming, that is, that he was still alive then; did you say something, Bill?"

"No, sir."

"Right, between 11:00 P.M. and 12:15 and, provided your theory about the window is correct, suspects can be limited to the professor, Miss Makepeace, Ms. Moore"—Grant gave the prefix a slight, derisory emphasis—"Mr. Wyndham, Mr. Childe, Miss Stainmore and Miss Lisle."

William waited quietly, knowing by now when his superior officer required silence. Grant considered the pattern of his socks then asked, "What is your opinion of Professor Turvey and Miss Lisle?"

"I found Turvey's concern over the fate of the symposium in the face of his co-founder's death excessive. It suggests little love lost between the two of them and an involvement with the society that goes beyond the normal. As to Miss Lisle"—William paused then continued smoothly—"she seemed an honest witness, conscientious in her account, not considering that she herself could be a suspect. She also makes the best kedgeree I have ever tasted." He could have added that he thought she was the most sympathetic female he had met in a long time and also one of the most attractive, but he didn't.

"And what of the others?"

"Come, sir, you can't ask me to comment on them at this stage, I've hardly met them."

"I think you can," insisted Grant, "we breakfasted with them after all. Interesting, wasn't it, how those staying in the main building, our circle of suspects as you would consider them, all sat together?"

"People at occasions like this always break into natural groups early on, it's like being on-board ship," said William. "I think it's more interesting that we chose to sit with them rather than some of the others." He thought for a moment then started, a little reluctantly, "Charles Childe seems a bit of a joke, the way he came downstairs with his hand in a sling expecting to be the star turn and was then so put out to find he'd been upstaged by Cary's death. Gray Wyndham I found something of a mystery man. He seems to be different from the rest—he was the only one who paid no attention to what he was eating. He consumed that kedgeree as though it was a bowl of cereal." William was still shocked at the memory.

"Miss Makepeace seems a straightforward countrywoman but one with intelligence, she could be interesting to get to know. Miss Stainmore appears to be a typical, highly strung, rather pretentious member of the media. I'm afraid I can't remember much about Ms. Moore other than that wonderful mop of red hair and a charming Irish accent. Probably older than she looks at first glance," he added as an afterthought.

Grant twirled a pencil in his fingers absent-mindedly for a moment then said, "You're a sophisticated sort of chap, Bill, eat out at the best restaurants and all that, what do you think of a group of people who come to spend an entire weekend guzzling funny dishes and talking about ancient recipes?"

William looked slightly shocked and when he spoke his voice was defensive. "Judging by what we've heard, sir, and that breakfast"—he still couldn't forget the kedgeree—"the food could hardly be called funny. I don't know much about the history of gastronomy but I suppose it's a discipline like any other. Like archaeology, for instance; perhaps that's why Professor Turvey is so involved."

"Oxbridge graduates would stick together." Grant's voice was far

from affectionate. William sighed and wondered how long it would
be before he was in a position to bully subordinates to compensate
for his hang-ups, then immediately took back the thought. Grant
didn't bully, most of the time he was extremely fair. Perhaps, William thought, he himself was a little ultra-sensitive on certain points?
He brought his mind back to the problem in hand; Grant was asking
him something. "How tall would you say Cary was?"

William flicked through his notebook, "Six foot four, sir."

"Couple of inches taller than you, eh?"

William nodded.

"Stand up." As Grant spoke, he swung his legs off the table and
allowed his chair to settle back with a crash on the floor. He stood in
front of his sergeant, the top of his head coming little higher than
William Pigram's chin. The slight, dapper figure stepped back a
pace, aimed his pencil, then made a stabbing motion into William's
upper body. The point of the pencil prodded the sergeant's stomach
in the region of his navel. William flinched slightly from the force of
the attack.

"What does that suggest to you, Bill?"

"The murderer was probably a good bit taller than you, sir."

Grant sat down again, without putting his legs back on the table,
and waited.

"Turvey's the same height as myself, and so, more or less, is
Wyndham."

"And?" prompted Grant.

"Miss Lisle is nearly as tall." William forced his voice to rise above
a mutter.

"And is a cook with a cook's strong arms and skill with knives."

William sensibly remained silent. By now, he thought, he should
have trained himself not to allow personal feelings to affect his reaction to possible suspects in a crime case but there were occasions
when it still proved extremely difficult.

Grant made some notes in a little book lying on the desk in front
of him. "Arrange for someone to check out Cary's home, the address
will be in that file Turvey gave us. I understand he's a widower and
Miss Lisle says she is his only relative. Tell them to check for details
of any close friends, see what they can find out about his background, particularly anything linking him with any of the people

here. And get the home telephone number of Cary's newspaper editor, he may be able to tell us something about him.

"With the knife left in situ, there's hardly any blood, so little use looking for bloodstained clothing, but make a note to check what everyone was wearing last night just in case." He got up. "We'll look at that window now. If you're right about the angle of view it gives into the room, we can dismiss those symposiasts staying in the annexe and clear the ground for concentrating on the others." He paused, then gave Pigram a sardonic look. "Cheer up, it's always possible Cary could have been sitting down when he was stabbed."

Grant left the room, followed by a hot and angry William.

TEN

Darina worked in the kitchen preparing lunch. A cook is more conscious than most that the show must go on. Wherever a number of people are gathered together food will be required sooner or later. With her was her assistant, who had first been refused entry, then allowed into the hall and finally given clearance to report to the kitchen. Never talkative, Frances was shocked into almost total silence. Darina, who normally hated conversation whilst she was working and had sacked more than one assistant for an inability to get on with the job without a stream of chatter, for once would have welcomed some distraction from her thoughts.

"Murdered, murdered," ran the refrain in her head. Someone had murdered Digby. "Dead, Digby dead," counterpointed another little refrain. Her charismatic cousin, who had thrown a shadowy cloak of influence over most of her life, was gone. The man who had both attracted and repelled her was no more. Murdered. Someone had murdered Digby.

Nicholas could avoid facing the awkward fact if he liked, but Darina had never flinched from unpalatable truths and the one sticking out at her like a shop-bought cake in a farmhouse spread, was that the someone had to be one of the symposiasts. The chance of an outsider entering the abbey at dead of night to murder Digby was so remote Darina refused to consider it. No, it must surely be one of them. And one of those staying in the abbey itself rather than the annexe. For Darina's thoughts had moved with the same cool logic as those of the detectives.

Who could have wanted to do away with Digby and why? As she unmoulded game pies, pulled apart roasted free-range chickens, made cucumber sauce and arranged small savoury tarts on plates, Darina reflected that many people could have wished her cousin

dead. He had wielded power in the food world. He had made and
broken careers. And there had been more than a few jealous comments in her hearing last year, when little was known of her connection with Digby. There were many who had no cause to thank him.
Many who itched to replace him in one of the many niches he occu-
pied: cookery columnist in newspapers and magazines, restaurant
reviewer, demonstrator at prestigious events, presenter of food programmes on TV and radio, endorser of a select range of products;
Darina could foresee a rush of candidates to fill the vacant spots
created by his death.

In his personal life, too, Digby had attracted enemies like a treacle
tart the flies. His many affairs and liaisons had left a trail of jealous
husbands and abandoned lovers. How many of them had vowed
vengeance? Was one of them amongst the symposiasts staying in the
abbey?

But murder . . . who would go to such lengths? What extremity
of hate or bitterness was required to bring a person to kill? Darina
thought of the sharp, thin boning knife, imagined deliberately picking it up and plunging it into Digby's chest.

"Are you all right?" asked Frances anxiously.

Darina swallowed hard. There were beads of cold sweat on her
forehead. She grabbed a piece of kitchen paper and pressed it to her
face.

"Stop for a minute and have a cup of coffee, there's some left over
from this morning."

Darina allowed herself to be sat down and took the mug gratefully.
It had been hours since she and Nicholas had shared coffee waiting
for the police to arrive. Time since then had been confused. Breakfast had come and gone. Frances and she had served coffee to the
police and officials taking fingerprints, brief statements and details
from the bewildered symposiasts, and turning over the housekeeper's
room with the efficiency of food inspectors searching for cock-
roaches. And she'd given her statement to the two policemen in
charge.

They'd questioned her with unnerving politeness. She'd told her
story as simply and directly as she could, and there'd been little need
for questions from the dapper man who sat behind the table and
watched her with detached eyes, occasionally making a note in a

neat, crabbed hand in a small ring-book in front of him. The younger man had taken down everything she said. At the end he'd given her an encouraging smile. In other circumstances she might have found his thin, intelligent face and shock of dark, curly hair attractive. As it was, he had asked the one question she didn't want to answer.

"Do you know any reason why anyone should want to murder your cousin, Miss Lisle?"

Did she know any reason? Miss Makepeace calling for justice to be brought down on Digby rose before her. Miss Makepeace whose passion was the history of food, who thought her book had been stolen and who looked as though she wouldn't hurt a fly.

"No," Darina had said steadily, "there were a number of people who didn't particularly like him, but I don't know anyone who would kill him."

If that was a specious answer, they didn't question it.

Sitting down sipping her coffee, Darina saw two pairs of legs walk past the high, narrow window that did its best to illuminate the kitchen, without great success. Even on the brightest day it was necessary to have the strip lighting on. How had they managed in the days before electric lights, she wondered.

Darina finished her coffee and got up, saw the legs return, then the two detectives bend down and peer into the room, crouching like frogs about to leap a lily-pad. She repressed an urge to make a silly face and started preparing a salad from John Evelyn's seventeenth-century *Acetaria*.

"Have you seen my rubber gloves?" she asked Frances a moment later. "I'm sure I left them beside the sink last night, now I can't find them anywhere."

"I haven't had them, or seen them. There's a new pair under the sink, though."

Darina opened the sink cupboard door, put on the new gloves and started scrubbing celery.

Ten minutes later Nicholas came in, flushed and angry. "The police have told all the symposiasts staying in the annexe to go home!" He seemed almost on the verge of tears. "They say the symposium can't go on. And those of us staying in the abbey have to remain for further questioning—it's too much!"

Darina looked at the array of food, lunch for forty-plus people. "Are they allowed to eat before they leave?"

"I insisted, that's what I've come to tell you. Can you serve it immediately? The inspector says they want them gone within the hour."

Lunch was not the relaxed, chatty meal that had been intended. Instead of happy symposiasts discussing the morning's proceedings, exchanging theories and gossiping, the refectory split into two quite different groups. Those staying in the annexe were noisy and excited, full of the thrill of being involved in a major event without the threat of serious side-effects. Nicholas moved amongst them, giving assurances of information on a new date for the symposium as soon as possible and murmuring something about refunds.

Sitting quietly together was the group staying in the abbey itself. There was little animation here. Gray sat calmly eating and reading the morning paper, seemingly unaffected by the drama. Miss Makepeace made the odd note in her little book but her usual concentration had gone. The pudding bowl haircut had odd strands sticking out as though she'd stirred it with her pencil. She glanced round the room every so often but hardly seemed to register what she saw. She looked as though she was rather gazing inwards and was troubled at what she found.

Linda had initially brought a plate of salad to the same table, but barely had she sat than she darted up at the sight of the inspector coming into the room. After an urgent little conversation, he had shrugged his shoulders and nodded reluctantly, then caught her arm and uttered a few crisp words more before she moved swiftly out of the refectory and he continued on his way through to the kitchen.

Charles Childe sat sulkily nursing his wounded hand, ostentatiously carried in a large sling made from a paisley silk scarf. Rita seemed to have appointed herself guardian angel, bringing him plates of food, tucking a napkin under his chin and cutting up his meat. The skin around her eyes was puffy as though she had been crying.

"Maybe I shouldn't say this," said Charles as Darina brought over a plate of cold venison, "but I can't help wondering if Digby wrote up my restaurant before he"—the light voice hesitated for a moment—"before he met his tragic end," he finished, putting his fork down on an almost empty plate. "It's unforgivable of me, of course, thinking of myself at a time like this, but it could mean so much to me." He looked anxiously around the little group. "A really good review, and I'm sure Digby wouldn't have given us anything else, would bring people flocking to Wandsworth."

"Miss Lisle!" It was the inspector, back from the kitchen with the tall sergeant at his heels. "We'd like a few more words with you, please."

Darina felt an unpleasant lurch to her stomach. "Certainly, Inspector, I'll just tell Frances to serve coffee to those who have to stay. And what about your men, do you think they'd like some lunch, there's plenty left." She indicated the still-laden table.

Sergeant Pigram brightened. "How kind, would you like me to organise that, sir?"

"And what about yourselves?" asked Darina as Grant nodded. "Shall I bring you a tray?"

"We'll wait," he said briefly, ignoring the look shot him by his sergeant, and went on his way.

As she turned to go to the kitchen, Darina caught a glimpse, out of the long refectory windows, of Linda leading her television team up to the front door. A departing symposiast was stopped and questioned, camera whirring happily. So, persistence had won permission for them to film after all. The image of carrion crows picking at slaughtered wildlife slipped into Darina's mind.

ELEVEN

As Darina came into the writing room a few minutes later, Grant was replacing the telephone receiver, the installation of which had been achieved a couple of hours earlier. He sat in an easy chair by the side of the writing table but quickly rose and pulled out the chair opposite the table.

"Please sit down, Miss Lisle. Ah, Bill, got the ravening hordes to the trough, have you? Why don't you conduct this interview?"

William closed the door behind him and came forward cursing under his breath. Normally he was delighted when Grant allowed him to interview witnesses, it gave him an agreeable sensation of progress in his career. But this time he would far rather have taken the notes. Or would he? He suddenly realised Grant was allowing him to set the pace, create the atmosphere he felt most conducive to eliciting the maximum amount of information from this witness. He would be in control, not Grant. But Grant would be sitting there, liable to take over the questioning at any time if he felt it required a new direction.

William sat down behind the table and got out his notebook. "Now, Miss Lisle, I want to go back to the incident of the dog."

"The dog that did bark," murmured Darina and he looked up with interest and pleasure. The witness was self-possessed and versed in Sherlock Holmes, or had she just been watching television?

"Quite. You stated that after you had become involved in the dog fight, Professor Turvey and Rita Moore came out of their rooms. What about Miss Stainmore and Miss Makepeace?"

"They must have been asleep."

"How much noise was there? You said your room was on the second floor; would you have woken up had you been asleep?"

"The dog's bark was very penetrating and Charles was really

screaming but I can't say whether it would have woken me up, I wasn't asleep."

"Where are Miss Stainmore and Miss Makepeace's rooms?"

"Linda is on the first floor, at the end of the west corridor. Miss Makepeace is on the second floor like me—there is a bathroom between our rooms, we share it."

"Would the noise have reached the kitchen?"

"I wouldn't have thought so, it wasn't that loud; the walls are all very thick and the sound would have had to travel through the refectory and down the stairs."

William made some notes then looked up. "How well did you know the deceased?" he asked smoothly.

He watched Darina's eyes widen slightly before she answered steadily, "As I told you, Digby was my cousin. His parents were both killed in a car crash when Digby was about seventeen. My father became his guardian and he spent his holidays with us until he left school, so he was almost a brother."

"And what happened then?"

"He had a year in France but we saw a lot of him when he was at university for a couple of years. Then he left, said academic life wasn't for him. Father got him a job as a trainee in one of the big London hotels; Digby thought he might like to become a manager. He was supposed to spend two years in the kitchens before moving on to other departments but after about eighteen months he decided it wasn't what he wanted after all and got himself a job in the public relations department of a food firm. We'd still seen quite a bit of him, he'd come down when a change in shifts meant he could have more than a day off. But just after he changed jobs, my father died and he got involved in London life and his visits somehow ended . . ." Darina's voice trailed away slightly.

She's still hurt about that, decided William. "How old were you when your father died?"

"Fifteen."

"And Digby Cary?"

"Oh, he must have been about twenty-four or twenty-five."

"When did you catch up with your cousin again?"

"About seven years ago. I'd done a year's cookery course and after that I worked in a local restaurant. Then someone offered me a job in a directors' dining room in London. The money was quite good and I thought if I also did dinner parties in the evenings, I could afford to share a flat with some girls I knew. Before I arrived, I wrote to Digby and told him I was coming, I thought it would be nice to see him again."

William watched a rosy blush colour her face and wondered what that letter had cost her to write. "How many years was it since you had seen him?"

"Just over six. He'd got married in the meantime. We were asked to the wedding, it was a very large one, Sarah had a title, her father was a marquis and she was the Lady Sarah something or other. I was quite keen to go but my mother wasn't very well at the time. Anyway, I got a very nice letter from Sarah after I'd written, saying she'd always wanted to meet Digby's only surviving relation and why didn't I come to Sunday lunch as soon as I arrived in London. So I did and after that I went there quite often." Darina paused. When she continued it was slowly as though, William thought, she was picking her way through a minefield.

"Sarah and I became very good friends. Digby often wasn't there, he was getting on very well in the food world, always having to go to food presentations, or receptions and things. He was freelancing with his public relations and writing on food for a small chain of provincial newspapers. He was also appearing on local television, demonstrating dishes. His career just took off and it wasn't long before he had a regular monthly column in a magazine and then a weekly one in a newspaper. He was always saying he had to make the most of every opportunity, which meant he often had to be away from home."

"It must have been lonely for his wife," commented William.

Darina made a neat pleat in the skirt of her overall and studied the result. "Sarah was a very self-sufficient person," she said at last, "and she was very proud of Digby's success."

She's hiding something, William said to himself. Who is it she is being loyal to, the husband or the wife? He felt the frisson of excitement that always came with identification of evasion in a witness.

"Did Cary help you in your career?"

"Occasionally he gave my name to hostesses who wanted a dinner party or a buffet and sometimes he used me to test recipes. Then last year he suggested to Nicholas that I should help with the food for the first symposium of the society."

She's relieved I've got off the subject of his marriage, William decided, and I don't think what she wants to hide has anything to do with this weekend.

"Did you see much of him on his own, professionally, as you might say?" The question was deliberately ambiguous and he held his breath for her answer.

Once again the blush coloured Darina's face. "Not very much. I found," she swallowed hard, "I found we no longer had so much in common." She stared out of the window at a garden made dreary by the fine rain. "He seemed to have changed since the time he lived with us."

Was he trying to make her on the side? William wondered.

"How would you describe yourself professionally, Miss Lisle?" Grant shot in the question and Darina turned in surprise. It was obvious she had forgotten the inspector sitting to one side of the writing table, out of her line of sight but able to watch her face as she answered the sergeant's questions. She hesitated.

"I mean, are you an outside caterer, a cook, a cordon bleu artiste, or what?"

She laughed at that, a delightfully frank and open laugh. "Oh, I see what you mean. I always just say I'm a cook, ready to tackle any cooking assignment."

"Have knife, will travel?" For a moment William had lost sight of the purpose of the interview. A shadow fell over Darina's face and Grant stirred with annoyance. "I'm sorry, that was tactless of me," William apologised, but the damage was done; the girl had lost the relaxation that had come as the questions turned away from Digby Cary.

"Do you make a reasonable living from your cooking?" Grant asked.

"Enough for most of what I want." There was no evasiveness in the answer.

"What are your plans for the future?"

Darina looked at the inspector in surprise. "Digby asked me that only last night."

"And what did you reply?"

"That I'd like to have my own hotel," she sighed, "but it's only a pipe-dream."

"Why?"

"I'd never be able to afford it." She was clearly astonished they couldn't work that out for themselves.

"Then you have seriously thought about it?" There was an edge of antagonism in Grant's voice, and William wondered where he was leading. There were times, he thought, when his superior made a religion of thinking the worst of people. Whilst such deep cynicism meant no possible nefarious motive could be overlooked, it made for hard going with the innocent. Then he caught himself up; why was he so sure this witness *was* innocent?

"I've thought about it, why not? A suitable property came on the market down here a little time ago. I did a budgeting exercise and went to see my bank manager, who explained in words of one syllable why my projected cash flow could hardly finance the loan, let alone provide me enough to live on." Was that bitterness in her voice or just deep disappointment? "So now I only fantasise about my hotel."

"You don't anticipate getting hold of sufficient money to make it a reality?" Grant persisted. "What about now your cousin is dead? You were his only relative, you said."

"I am, but I don't imagine Digby has left me anything."

"So it would be a surprise for you to learn that you are the sole legatee of his estate?"

Darina was not the only one to look at him in astonishment. It was news to William as well. So that was what had been behind Grant's questioning. The team at Cary's house must have uncovered that little nugget.

"I don't believe you," Darina said.

"The will was dated eight years ago; I imagine that was when he got married?" Darina nodded dumbly. Grant glanced down at his notebook. "It leaves everything to his wife in the first place, then, in the event of her predeceasing him, to any children; finally, in the event of there being no offspring, to 'my cousin, Darina Lisle.' That is you, I take it?"

William studied the shocked girl. Either the will was as much news to her as it was to him or she was a most accomplished actress.

Grant seemed unimpressed. "Money is one of the most powerful motives for murder and you seem to have benefited from Mr. Cary's death. By how much, I wonder?"

Darina looked down at her hands, tightly clasped in her lap, then back at the inspector. "I don't know but I think it could be quite a lot. Sarah had money, you see, and it was all left to Digby when she died about a year ago. She had already given him the house in Chelsea as a wedding present." Her grey eyes had grown enormous and the skin seemed to have tightened over the finely chiselled cheekbones. Her mouth was tense, but under Grant's searching gaze her chin rose a couple of inches.

"You think I did it, don't you?" Her voice was level and steady. "And I don't suppose it would carry much weight if I assured you I didn't. Digby and I didn't always see eye to eye but I certainly wouldn't murder him."

"And what didn't you always see eye to eye about?" enquired Grant smoothly. William knew he was not going to get the questioning back now; Darina was on her own.

Once again there was a fatal hesitation. "I didn't always approve of certain of his actions."

"What actions, Miss Lisle?"

"Nothing that has any bearing on this case, Inspector." There was a note of iron in Darina's voice.

"Perhaps you will tell us again just what happened last night, in every detail."

Darina stared at Grant then started to repeat the story of her actions the previous evening after Digby had asked her to tell Nicholas where he was, ending with her discovery of his body that morning.

After she stopped speaking, Grant said nothing and for several minutes they sat and looked at each other.

It was Darina who broke the silence. "There's something else," she said slowly. "I picked up the murder weapon. I told you I thought the boning knife was missing from the display—well, that was the one I examined when Digby was setting them out. The murderer has probably wiped the handle clean but there may well be an identifiable print on the blade." She grew even paler but her gaze didn't waver.

"That could be a very sensible statement or a very clever one." Grant spoke unemotionally. Darina sat silent and after another moment he said, "All right, Miss Lisle, you can go now. But don't leave the grounds of the abbey centre, we may wish to talk to you again." Without a glance at either of them, Darina rose and left the room. There was a sharp click as the door closed. Then Grant said, "Well, Bill, can you manage to see anything but outraged innocence there?"

"There's something she's hiding about her cousin and his wife."

"And what's your theory on that?"

"He could have been making advances to her."

"And him with a rich and titled wife. Hmm, I don't go for Amazons myself but our cook has a definite charm. And how do you think cookie responded? A quick jump into the bed of the cousin she hero-worshipped, whatever she says now about not seeing eye to eye with him? And then what? He grows tired of her, worries the affair's too near home, with her a friend of his wife and all? He drops her. She's bitter, frustrated and unable to pursue her hotel dreams. Perhaps she saw the weekend as her perfect opportunity to pick up the affair and tried to renew their relationship after dinner last night, perhaps even wanted him to marry her. He refused. Her life is blighted, she is holding the knife, so . . ." Grant made a graphic little gesture with his hand, driving home an imaginary knife. William winced.

"I don't think so, sir," he said carefully. "I think it more likely that she refused his advances. I think she is trying to hide something about the marriage, not her own part in it. We need to know more about the wife."

"Ah, now there I have an advantage over you. I finally managed to get hold of Cary's newspaper editor. He's badly shaken by the news. I gather Cary really was a star writer and will take some replacing. The editor knew them both quite well. It seems Cary landed a plum, one of the really loaded aristocracy, the Lady Sarah Knapp. Died a year ago of cancer of the pancreas, leaving a tidy little sum to her dearly beloved husband. How long he would have remained that if she had lived appears to be an interesting question. The editor was unusually circumspect for a newspaper man but I got the distinct impression that the deceased was quite a lad with the ladies."

"I suppose there's no doubt that she did die of cancer?"

"Bill, Bill!" Grant shook his head in mock despair. "Do you want to turn the deceased into a murderer? Or are you suggesting Miss Lisle first killed off the Lady Sarah and then Digby Cary so she could inherit all? You could have a point, make a note for Monday to look into the possibility."

William obediently scribbled in his book but he would bet his Dr. Johnson first-edition dictionary it was an avenue that would lead nowhere.

Grant arranged one leg over the other and thrust his hands into his pockets, gazing out of the window and thinking deeply. His thoughts were interrupted by the telephone. "Yes, what have you found now? . . . Have you indeed, and what does it say?" Grant made some rapid notes in his little ring-book. "Thanks. Let me know if you come across anything else interesting." He put the receiver back and looked across at William, his eyes alight. "That was the team at Cary's house. They've found a copy of the wife's will. What do you think it said?" Grant pushed across his ring-book so the sergeant could read his notes.

William studied the book with rising hope. "Well, sir, I think that sorts out the identity of our next witness, doesn't it?"

Grant nodded, "Go get him, Bill."

TWELVE

Darina closed the door of the incident room, walked rapidly through the hall for a few paces, then stopped.

She could hardly think straight. They actually seemed to believe she had murdered Digby. A long shudder ran through her and she looked round about her like a blind person searching for a source of light to orientate himself. Then she ran up the stairs to her room, grabbed a raincoat, ran down again and let herself out of the front door.

There was no television team outside. Whilst she'd been undergoing that rigorous questioning, the symposiasts had departed. The drive was bare and empty. A gust of rain lashed at her but the wind was light and the rain almost warm. The air still held a hint of the heat of late summer rather than the chill of winter to come. It felt fresh and clean and gentle. Darina stood on the wide step and breathed deeply. She felt she was emerging from a tortuous journey to a foreign land, the neat rose beds, damp lawns and thick hedges of shrubs taking on the dearly familiar look of home to a returning argonaut.

She raised the collar of her trench-coat, thrust her hands deep into her pockets and set out across the lawns, her sensible cook's shoes making light of the rain-sodden grass. As she walked, she went back over the interview, reliving the moment it became clear to her that she was under suspicion. Then she thought of her fingerprints on the knife. Thought of the incredible fact that Digby had left her all his money, tried to think how these facts might look to the police. Tried to remember what she had told them about her relationship with Digby. And reluctantly came to the conclusion that, had she been in their place, she might also think that Darina Lisle could be guilty.

Unbelievably, she was chief suspect in a murder case.

Darina continued walking and thinking. Most of the abbey land lay behind the main building and she followed the drive round the side of the old house, past the kitchen entrance, to where the few remaining cars were parked on a large expanse of tarmac. Stretching behind the abbey and connected by a covered walkway was the annexe, a plain and relatively unobtrusive building. Its red brick was darkened by the rain and several lights shone pale gold. Through the gloom of the afternoon, Darina noticed a number of people through one of the downstairs rooms. The television team had found a refuge.

The other side of the car-park was bounded by a large hedge of macrocarpa. Darina went through an arch in its centre and paused. To her left stretched the formal garden of rose bushes, to her right the lawn rolled over a bank then ran into rough grass and a shrubbery.

She turned right and plunged down the bank, letting the wind blow through a few loose wisps of hair. On an impulse, she reached up and removed the butterfly clip that held back the heavy fall, letting it hang free. Wind stirred the wings of hair then blew handfuls across her face, obstructing her vision and filling her mouth with damp-tasting strands.

Sighing, she retrieved the clip from her pocket and tried to recapture the errant locks.

"Need any help?" Gray had emerged from the shrubs at the bottom of the slope.

"It's just this stupid hair."

"Don't you dare call it stupid, it's glorious." He came round and captured the windswept tresses, holding them whilst Darina slipped the clip back into place.

"Thank you, now I can see again." She turned to face him. He stood relaxed, his eyes calm and questioning. To her dismay, she could feel tears pricking at hers.

He put a hand on her shoulder. "Something's upset you, is it those damned policemen?"

She tried to smile but found the sudden sympathy unlocked the tears. She brushed them aside with an angry gesture that knocked his arm away. "It's nothing. It just seems they've decided I'm number-one suspect."

"You! You can't be serious. What on earth makes them think something so entirely idiotic?"

His patent astonishment was bracing. Darina dug out a handkerchief and blew her nose with determination.

"Come on, let's walk down towards the lake whilst you tell me all about it. I thought that wretched hound was following me but he seems to have lost himself."

The wind bending the topmost branches and making a continuous backdrop of sound, they walked through the overgrown and tangled shrubbery, whilst Darina gave Gray an account of her interview.

"I suppose it does look rather black," she ended miserably, "and of everyone, I had the best opportunity."

"You mean," Gray spoke slowly, "they're basing their case on the fact that Digby left you all his money?"

She nodded. "And I didn't even know about his will but they don't believe me. It must be quite a lot of money," she added miserably.

The path had wound its way through the thick shrubs, at times so narrow they had to walk in single file, until it arrived at the edge of a small lake, a dark expanse of water rippling with wind and ringed with rhododendrons, viburnums and a few soaring pines. A path ran round it and where they stood was a small clearing, the ground springy and strewn with pine needles.

They looked across the lake, the light, slanting rain pitting its surface. "It's not as much as they think," said Gray, "and if that's their case, they'll have to add me to the top of the list with you."

Darina looked at him in astonishment.

"You never saw Sarah's will?" Darina shook her head. "She left her estate in trust, Digby was only to enjoy the income and after his death it was to go either to their children or to me and my heirs."

"You?" Darina could not work out the connection.

Gray picked up a stone and threw it across the water, making it skip towards the island, adding little, ever widening circles to the ruffled surface of the water.

"And money wouldn't have been my only motive." Gray studied the path of the stone, his face set and hard. "In a way you and I are sort of related—Sarah was *my* cousin."

As Darina continued to look at him, light dawned. "You're G.G.!" His face relaxed for a moment, became rueful. "My full name is Gray George. When she was a baby, Sarah couldn't manage Gray so I was called G.G. and the name stuck. She mentioned me to you, then?" He had the pleased look of a schoolboy whose essay has got top marks.

"Oh yes, constantly. She was always trying to drag you up to London." Darina cut herself short. Sarah had wanted her real cousin to meet her cousin-in-law because, she told Darina, she was match-making. Darina, bruised by the end of her affair with Jack, had laughed and told her that sort of planning never came off and after a little Sarah had seemed to drop the idea.

"I went to London once or twice when they were first married but I soon stopped." Deep anger ran beneath Gray's even tone. "I just couldn't take the way Cary treated her, leaving her for nights on end whilst he went off to do God knew what—" He broke off suddenly and reached for another stone. Darina waited.

"I loved her, you see," he continued after he had watched the second stone's path across the lake. "We more or less grew up together. My mother was widowed when I was a baby. My father ran through her money with an ease that amounted to genius, then finished off his life under a power boat water-skiing in the Mediterranean. My uncle, the marquis, came to her rescue, gave her Dorrington Dower House for her lifetime, and now allows me to live in a tiny cottage not far from there. I'm the poor relation that has to be looked after." There was a bitter twist to his mouth. "I spent most of my childhood with Sarah and her brother, Julius, the present marquis. He and I are practically twins, Sarah was a couple of years younger. Julius and I went to Eton together, courtesy of my uncle"—again the bitter twist—"then Julius went to agricultural college and I went up to Oxford. I actually won a scholarship there *and* qualified for a grant.

"After my degree I went on to work for a Ph.D. on the Gunpowder Plot. Fool that I was, I wanted to be in a position to offer Sarah some worldly goods of my own before asking her to marry me. It never occurred to me she wouldn't wait. Just as it looked as if I was on the path to fortune, when a biography of Guy Fawkes I'd written at the same time as my thesis became a popular success, she met

Digby." By now there was a depth of bitterness in his voice that was shocking. It was as if his anger and disappointment were turned as much against himself as Digby.

"So you didn't see much of her after they married?"

"Not in London but, as you probably know, Sarah would come down to Dorrington when Digby took off on his trips. We'd ride together and try to recapture the old days. But it always ended in my tackling her about Digby and finally we quarrelled. I was trying to make her leave him and she said I'd never understand and why didn't I leave her alone, it was her life." Emotion shook his voice. "She didn't come again. Some months later, Julius told me she was ill and the outlook was pretty grim. I wrote and finally I had a note from her asking if I'd like to come and see her in hospital. God, I think that was the worst day of my life," he said, his voice breaking slightly.

Darina knew he was seeing again what she had seen, Sarah's gaunt figure, the cloud of dark hair raked to wisps by radiotherapy, her eyes sunk deep in a skeletal face, the fleshless fingers picking at an odd grape, all she seemed able to eat; only her smile was the same, yet not the same. How could it be the same when all else was so altered? Yet it held the quintessential Sarah, and her arms, those painfully bony arms, came up with the same warmth and her voice was as alive and caring as ever.

"She wouldn't hear a word against Digby," said Darina quietly. "When I cursed him for not visiting her more often, she said it wasn't because he didn't care but because the sight of her suffering upset him so much. She told me I must understand he wasn't as strong as I was, he'd always needed someone at his side who could be there without making demands or putting pressure on him. She'd said more or less the same earlier, when I told her she was a fool to put up with his treatment of her." Darina's voice was savage. "How do you think I felt, knowing it was *my* cousin treating her like that? Knowing that everywhere he went there was a 'little number'?

"But, Gray"—her voice changed—"whatever we felt about the situation, I really think she was happy with him. She didn't like parties and hated the crowds of people Digby throve on, she preferred to stay at home. And he did care for her. You didn't see them together as I did. We'd have supper, just the three of us, and it was such fun, trying out Digby's new recipes, him telling us what was going on in the food world, Sarah teasing him and making extremely perceptive comments. Or we'd go to a new restaurant, I would book the table in my name and often Digby wouldn't be recognised, he knew how to tone down his personality when he really wanted to be incognito. Then we'd go back home and dissect the food and he'd make notes for his restaurant column. He could be absolutely savage in his reviews but sometimes, if the food wasn't as good as he felt it should have been but he liked the chef or the owner, he'd be very amusing and make you want to go and try it for yourself. They were good evenings." Darina paused, remembering those times before Digby had made the final betrayal.

"Sarah said to me once," she continued with an effort, feeling she had to make Gray understand, "that if I ever fell deeply in love and knew that I was needed by the person I loved, I wouldn't care about his shortcomings. I would be happy knowing I was making his life comfortable and he was happier for my being there. I think she really believed that, she was a most remarkable person."

Darina fell silent. They both looked at the lake, its bleakness under the grey sky matching the bleakness of their mood.

"You're very different from Cary," said Gray at last, "so restful, I feel I've known you for years. You must take after the parent that wasn't related to him."

"I'm not like my mother at all," said Darina, amused, "and she wouldn't thank you for suggesting I was. No, I take after Father. But Digby's mother wasn't like him. Father was very sensible and logical. I gather she was all emotion and would never listen to reason, a bit like my mother, in fact. She married, as they used to say, 'beneath her.'

"Digby's father was my grandparents' gardener, very attractive physically but not much upstairs. I think Digby's mother got pregnant and insisted on marriage. They had no money, he was found a job that carried a cottage and she was given a little car and a tiny income. It was very different from what she had been used to. I don't think she had any inner resources and he forgot any conversation he'd ever had, so she turned to drink. My grandmother set up a trust fund to pay for Digby's schooling. My father never had much spare cash, my mother is expensive, but he used to send the odd cheque for Digby's clothes, though I think it often bought whisky rather than trousers.

"Digby grew up an awful snob. I think he was almost relieved when his parents were killed in that car crash and he could come and live with us. He considered a settled, middle-class home with a respectable doctor as uncle-guardian a considerable improvement on his previous situation. He took years to appreciate vegetables." Darina thought for a moment, then added, "It's little wonder that, as soon as he could, Digby gravitated to the beautiful people—the rich, the well-connected, the powerful—and strove to become one himself. But what Sarah saw was the little boy who'd never found tea ready when he came home from prep school, whose father never prepared him for life, whose mother never darned his socks, who needed constant reassurance that he could be loved simply for what he was."

There was a silence. Whilst they'd been talking, the rain had eased. There was a break in the heavy cloud then thin, silvery light slanted through, giving the shrubs extra depth and darkness. Darina shivered. "It seems to be getting chilly." She looked at the tall figure at her side. "Aren't you exhausted, you can't have got back until the early hours of this morning?"

"I should be, I suppose, it certainly took long enough for Childe's hand to be sewn up and then we had to wait whilst they organised medication but, funnily enough, I don't feel at all tired. We should be going back, though. Where's that damn dog got to? Bracken! Bracken!"

They listened. Nothing. Gray called again and then again. Finally, some way off, they heard a rustle which turned into a violent shaking of branches and leaves. There were a few happy yelps and Bracken erupted from dense ground cover, his tongue lolling out of his panting mouth, ears swept back, coat covered in burrs. He looked very happy, his sides heaving with the effort of getting his breath back. Darina leant down to pat him. "Good boy! What a clever boy to come when he's called."

"It's a miracle," Gray said dryly.

As he fastened the lead onto the dog's collar, Darina's eye was caught by his shirt cuff. "Has he bitten *you?*" she asked and when he looked bewildered, she pointed to the bloodstains on the cuff.

He studied them in surprise. "Must have come from Childe last night," he said finally. "I didn't even realise they were there." He drew his raincoat sleeve over the cuff and they started to walk back towards the abbey, the dog trotting quietly beside them.

As they emerged from the shrubbery, Sergeant Pigram came round the macrocarpa hedge and sighted them with all the enthusiasm of Cortez catching his first view of the Pacific.

"Mr. Wyndham! I've been searching for you everywhere, the inspector would like to see you immediately, please."

Gray sighed. "The inquisition starts! Have I time to return the dog to his dungeon?"

"I'll take him back if you like," offered Darina.

Gray handed over the lead. "Thanks, and if you could feed him as well, he'll be your friend for life. The tins and biscuits are on a table behind the door of the boiler room."

THIRTEEN

Darina took the dog in the back way. The door to the housekeeper's room was open. Grey powder obscured surfaces, and a photographer was bent over the table, capturing its maze of fingerprints. By Digby's writing table two men were carefully going through his files and boxes. On the floor was a chalk outline of a body with drawn-up leg and flung-out arm. Darina passed swiftly on.

As she filled the dog's bowl with food, she thought over the conversation with Gray. No wonder he had been so antagonistic towards Digby. If she had been bitter against her cousin for his treatment of Sarah, how much more so must he have been. Bitter enough to kill Digby? Or could he have killed for the money? Or both?

Controlling her instinctive flinching from the thought, she put the bowl on the floor and watched the dog wolf his food, sending her mind back to her conversation with his master the previous evening. Hadn't he said he'd come on the weekend to get background material for a novel which he hoped would make him some money?

What were his financial circumstances? He'd spoken about popular success and his clothes looked good if ancient, but it hadn't sounded as though he was able to escape from the charity of his rich relations.

What were the chances of his novel making real money? He'd surely have to be very lucky to hit the jackpot with his first attempt. Darina found it difficult to see the confused and emotionally innocent Gray pulling off a steamy success, and what other sort of book made money these days? Just how much did he need Sarah's trust fund?

With a little jolt, Darina realised that Gray's new fortune meant her chance of financial independence had been snatched away. But all she could feel was overwhelming relief. Not only had a motive for killing Digby gone but inheriting Sarah's money had not felt right.

The dog finished his meal and came and rubbed his head against Darina's leg. She gave him a quick pat and started to leave the room, then looked at the door. She tried closing it and noticed how the latch failed to click shut, bouncing back a little and leaving the door just proud of the architrave. Enough purchase for a dog's inquisitive nose to work on. She went outside and repeated the experiment, then waited. Almost immediately she could see the door move slightly and could imagine Bracken getting to work on releasing himself from his confinement. A few minutes later, an ecstatic dog was licking her hand. Feeling a traitor, she returned him to the room and made sure the door was securely latched before going across to the kitchen. She made some tea and took it through to an empty lounge, then returned to the kitchen to start preparing for the evening meal.

As she was securing the last of a series of pigeons in overcoats of blanched lettuce, Nicholas came in, fussily rustling through a sheaf of papers. "Darina, dear, what about dinner? Only a few of us, what a travesty of a gathering, but we have to eat."

"I'm preparing about half of the dishes we agreed and cutting down quantities," she said soothingly.

"Good, good. And you must eat with us; no, I insist. That admirable Frances can hold the fort here, surely. We need you, such a disparate little group, hardly a rational person amongst them. I except Linda, of course, so intelligent and enterprising. You know she has got the inspector to agree to her filming again? She's preparing a programme on Digby, his death and the investigation. We hope it will be a little memorial to him."

Darina noted the possessive pronoun with a little spurt of amusement.

"Of course, it's hardly the programme that was originally intended but it could generate interest in a rescheduling of the symposium."

What a change from his previous disdain of the media. Darina finished tying up the pigeon and asked, "What has everyone been doing? I put tea in the lounge a little while ago but no one was around."

"Miss Makepeace said she was going to work on her notes in her room. Linda, of course, is filming. Rita and I have been in the bar discussing the book she is working on, then Charles Childe appeared and announced he had a splitting headache and she went off to find him some aspirin. Really, he is a tiresome little man. Now I'm waiting to be called by the police, I expect to be their next interviewee." He made it sound a privilege. "Wyndham's in there at the moment. Why they should want to see him before me, I find it hard to imagine."

Darina explained Gray's connection with Digby whilst inwardly marvelling at an amour-propre that could demand a leading role in a murder investigation.

"Ah, yes, Wyndham's rich relations." There was a slight sneer in Nicholas's tone.

Darina studied him thoughtfully for a moment as he picked amongst the lettuce leavings for a juicy morsel to nibble on.

"Did Gray really have a great success with a book on Guy Fawkes?"

Nicholas looked up, a small piece of lettuce caught on his lower lip trembling tantalisingly as he spoke. "Oh, yes, it even crept into the lower reaches of the best-seller list. It made the most of the sensational aspects, of course. If it had come out before his thesis had been considered, we might have had serious doubts about his methodology. As it was, he had his doctorate and the offer of a post. Which he proceeded to turn down." Nicholas made it sound as if a football pool player had refused a first dividend. "He'd have had tenure by now." A first dividend of extraordinary proportions obviously.

"What has he written since?" Darina placed the neatly wrapped birds on a plate and started forming forcemeat into walnut-sized balls.

Nicholas reached for a piece of the finely minced mixture. "No more successes, that's for certain." He sounded unbearably smug. "Lost the touch. Tries for popular appeal but his subjects are all too obscure. If he'd only stayed with us, he might have done some proper work, have had a reputation by now. As it is . . ." The little wave of his hand, holding a large chunk of meat-ball, was contemptuously dismissive.

"What about the novel he's writing at the moment? The one you suggested the weekend might provide some background information for?"

"My dear, the poor fellow was so obviously struggling, I thought the symposium might be a useful distraction. And have you seen the old kitchen at Dorrington House? Perfect Victoriana. Hasn't been touched since the turn of the century. The family just installed a new one on the ground floor and gave the other over to storage and mice. Now if we could have a weekend there, or even a session, we could turn back the clock and get the old range going. There's even a Dutch oven and a bottle jack, plus the old spit mechanism. We could have meat roasted as it used to be, the outside crusted with its juices, the inside rare and succulent. And there's a bread oven. Think of the loaves, the meat pies, the baking you could produce from it." Nicholas's mouth was obviously watering at the prospect.

"Have you discussed it with Gray?"

Nicholas came back to earth. "Thought I would bring the matter up at the end of the weekend. Shall have to check they haven't done anything with it recently—must be nearly ten years since I saw it, Gray asked me to stay with him during a long vac one time and showed me all over the estate. There's a most interesting ruined ice-house in the grounds, beautifully sited, dug out of a north-facing slope and in the path of prevailing winds. Wouldn't need much restoration to make it usable. All you'd need then would be a snowy winter to pack it full of ice."

Darina wondered if Gray's real crime in Nicholas's eyes hadn't been a failure to make his family's culinary past available to his tutor. "Did you never discuss the possibility with Digby and Sarah?"

"Digby and Sarah?" Nicholas grew waspish again. "I was never on socialising terms with Digby, my dear. Our historical meals did not include spouses and hangers-on. No, I never even met Digby's wife. Nor was I aware of her connection with Dorrington." Another grievance to be laid at Digby's door.

"He didn't comment at Gray's joining the weekend?"

Nicholas popped a last piece of forcemeat into his mouth and picked up his sheaf of papers. "Digby's only interest in the list of those coming was to check the press. Dinner at 8:00 P.M.? Remember, you are to dine with us. Now, I'd better see if the police are ready for me."

He went out before Darina could tell him the piece of lettuce was still sticking to his lip.

She reached for a large casserole and started smearing butter generously over its bottom, her mind on the conversation. If she could rely on what Nicholas had said, and there seemed little reason to suppose he had materially distorted the truth, Gray was in a sad way. He had thrown away a chance of academic status and failed to make his name as a popular historian. Perhaps that explained some of his bitterness.

How galling, also, must have been Digby's success, especially if he'd been unaware of the hard work that lay behind the seeming ease with which Sarah's husband had made his way. Darina found herself shivering. Revenge and the opportunity of financial independence, all Gray's at the stroke of a knife.

The kitchen door swung open and the room suddenly filled with people. Linda came towards the table, her team of technicians busily setting up lights and checking camera angles.

"Would now be a convenient moment to get our shots of the kitchen and some cooking?" The question was thrown carelessly at Darina, eager agreement obviously anticipated; the producer's eyes were already clicking round the room, assessing shots and possible background features.

"I can't imagine why you need to film in here and it's certainly not convenient, it will get in the way of preparations for dinner," said Darina sharply.

"It's a weekend all about food, people came here to discuss, eat and look at food. Digby was murdered with a kitchen knife. You must see that not to film you and the kitchen would provide a totally unbalanced programme. OK?"

"You want to film me?" Darina was unprepared for this development.

"You are the cook, aren't you?" Linda was all weary patience. "Now, if you stand here, so we've got that nice dresser in the background, and be doing, what can you be doing, dear?" Her eye fell on the plate of wrapped birds. "What are these? . . . Pigeons in lettuce? And what is going to happen to them? . . . Right, that could be interesting. Can you undo that last one? OK. Derek, shot of me talking to Darina whilst she's tying it up."

Darina snipped away the threads from one of the birds, fuming at the calm takeover of her kitchen. There were moments of what seemed interminable waiting whilst lights were adjusted and camera angles tested; Linda scribbled little notes on her board then finally gave a signal to start the action.

"Darina Lisle, you are cooking the food for this weekend, is it a daunting task to produce recipes from the past?"

Rather to her surprise, Darina found her mind working smoothly, unphased by the bright lights and pressure of the turning camera.

"It's a nice challenge. I've had great fun searching through old recipe books to find suitable dishes and then experimenting with them."

"And what are you doing here?"

Darina's nimble fingers rapidly retied the bird as she explained it was to be braised with forcemeat balls and slices of bacon on a bed of boiled parsley and butter, then served garnished with lemon.

"It sounds delicious." Linda couldn't quite manage enthusiasm but her perfunctory note could be put down to the need to move on to the next shot. "What else are you doing for this evening's meal?"

"Well, we're going to start with oysters and livers grilled on skewers." A camera followed Darina to the larder as she collected another set of ingredients.

"Tell me, Darina, how did you become involved in this arcane food?"

"Digby Cary asked me to help the chief cook last year." Darina's fingers fumbled and she dropped an oyster. She stopped talking and concentrated on pushing bits of food onto the metal skewer.

"Did you know Digby well?"

Darina put down a loaded skewer and started on another. "He was my cousin," she said shortly and could sense Linda's interest level move into overdrive, but she remained silent and after a moment or two Darina felt she had to say something more. "I'm a freelance cook. Normally I do dinner parties, directors' lunches, wedding buffets, that sort of thing." Her voice became stronger. "I found last year fascinating and started to collect some old recipe books and experiment with the dishes. Then Digby suggested I might like to take over the food for this weekend."

"And now there's been this tragic murder. How you will miss him." Linda sounded a shade theatrical.

"He was a great cook." Darina couldn't think of anything else to say about her cousin, she felt inadequate and resentful at being put in this position. The cameras were still turning and Linda was still standing waiting for more.

"If there isn't anything else, I'll get on with the cooking," Darina said finally and moved deliberately over to the other end of the kitchen, taking the dish of pigeons with her.

"Fine, cut!" said Linda. "We can edit that into a usable minute or two. Pity, though, you couldn't say anything more about Digby, you must have known him better than anyone else on this weekend. Perhaps we can record another piece with you later on."

"I'd rather not," said Darina curtly.

"I'm sure you can manage a quick little bit, OK?" Linda made a note on her clipboard. "Now," she turned to the others, "let's see if we can get a shot of the scene of the murder."

She led the way out of the kitchen by the door next to the housekeeper's room, shutting it firmly behind her, and though Darina listened intently she was unable to hear anything of her confrontation with the police.

She started adding boiling stock to the dish of pigeons, then the kitchen door opened again and Linda marched back in, her cheeks flushed.

"No luck?" asked Darina cheerfully.

"Officious police! They don't seem to realise we can do them a lot of good. Television has such power. But they wouldn't listen to reason." Linda looked as though her confrontation had gone beyond reasonable discussion.

"Perhaps they're more worried about you destroying a clue. What have you done with your crew?"

"Oh, they've gone off home. There's no more filming we can do tonight." Linda perched herself on the corner of the kitchen table. The narrow little miniskirt she was wearing displayed an expanse of leg thin rather than slender. Trousers suited her better, thought Darina cattily, but could not fault the beautifully cut jacket that was a whisper shorter than the skirt.

"There's one more thing." Linda smoothed down her skirt. "I

wondered if you had a similar knife to the one used for the murder. I'd hoped to find one next door but the police are being very boring and unhelpful." She added a big smile by way of inducement.

Darina looked at her in silence for a moment. Linda seemed unaware she had asked for anything out of the ordinary.

There was little point in being squeamish, Darina decided. She went to her knife roll and picked out one with a sharp, narrow blade a little under six inches in length. "That is practically identical to the boning knife used to kill Digby," she said calmly. "Be careful with it, it's very sharp."

"I'm always careful," said Linda smugly and held it somewhat gingerly in her hand. She made an awkward sort of stabbing motion in the air. Darina took a pace back.

Linda practised a little, wristy movement with the knife, then placed it on the table beside her and looked down at it. "Can I borrow this until tomorrow so we can get a shot of it? You wouldn't like to demonstrate its use, I suppose?"

Darina shook her head firmly.

"I didn't think so." Linda picked up the knife and her clipboard and, holding both carefully, left the kitchen.

FOURTEEN

It was not until later that Darina found time to wonder once again about Gray. She left Frances in charge of the kitchen and went off to slip into a hot bath.

Soaping her long legs and overcoming a deep-seated reluctance even to contemplate the possibility, she seriously considered the question of whether he could be the murderer. He had motive, he had had opportunity. Just how long had it taken him to put the dog into the boiler room, without latching the door properly? Charles had certainly been got upstairs and Rita had washed his hand before Gray reappeared.

Then she had another thought. Could Gray have murdered Digby before he went for his walk? That would have given him more time. Time; how long does it take to kill someone? Do you have a long conversation first, tell them why, or do you just stick the knife straight in? But he couldn't have known the knives would be there, nobody knew the knives were there except herself and, maybe, Nicholas. Had Digby discussed the sale of the knives with him?

Except, then, for the possibility of Nicholas, no one would have gone to that room intending to kill Digby, at least not with a knife. It must have been unpremeditated.

Had there been an argument? Had Digby made someone so angry they'd picked up the nearest weapon and attacked him? Darina thought of Digby's bulk. Would someone Miss Makepeace's size, for instance, be capable of sticking a knife into someone so much larger than herself? Then she thought of Gray, only two inches or so shorter than Digby. Not nearly as heavy but wiry and looking quite strong. Nicholas was also tall.

Which brought her to the co-founder of the society. He had certainly shown himself resentful of Digby's success and the way he seemed to be taking over the society. And he had apparently wanted to discuss something with the chairman. Had he gone down to the housekeeper's room after all? If he had intended a short discussion over some detail of the weekend, the conversation could easily have developed into an argument over, say, the increased publicity and the way Digby seemed to be taking over all the decision-making.

As she let the bathwater out, Darina realised with some surprise that she had been thinking about the murder as a technical problem. It had separated itself from her personal feelings for Digby. But was it a problem for her? Darina considered the question and came to the conclusion it might be. Not only did the police seem to allot her the role of prime suspect, she discovered a sense of loyalty to Digby.

Despite everything that had passed between them, he had been her cousin, had meant a lot to her at one stage of her life. And he had had a right to his life. But what could she do? The job of finding murderers was one for the police.

Darina dressed in a navy blue silky knitted dress that skimmed the tops of her knees. Remembering Linda's miniskirt, she regretted it wasn't shorter, as her legs were one of her best features. She brushed the long, dark cream hair and fastened the strands back with a navy bow to match the dress, added a hint of eye make-up, applied pink lipstick, then picked up her overall, pausing for a final check in the mirror. It seemed to reflect not her image but Digby's, and behind him stood the shadowy shape of Sarah.

In her place, Sarah would make every effort to find Digby's killer. After all, how far were the police getting? If they were concentrating on her as chief murderer, not very far. And they didn't know Digby the way she had. Didn't know the weaknesses that could generate emotions in other people powerful enough to provoke murder. And what harm could it do to find out a little more about the others involved? With a satisfying sense of purpose, Darina left her room and went downstairs.

There was only one person in the bar. Seated in a chair by the door, a notebook at hand as always, was Miss Makepeace. She was making no attempt to study her notes—the book was not even open, her eyes were fixed on the window and whatever she was seeing, Darina was sure it was not the herbaceous border in its autumnal shades of auburn and gold.

"Good evening, Miss Makepeace, would you like a glass of wine?"

"Oh, Miss Lisle, I was miles away. How kind of you, yes, I would enjoy a glass of white wine. My sister and I always used to have a glass before our evening meal. We made it ourselves."

Darina poured out two glasses of dry white wine, making a note in a little book. The bar was run for the weekend on the honour principle, symposiasts helping themselves to drinks. One of the abbey staff cleared up and worked out the accounts from the bar entries.

Darina brought over the glasses and sat in the chair next to Miss Makepeace.

Short, blunt fingers took the glass, the brown eyes opaque behind the pebble lenses.

"I unnerstand you have had two interviews with the police," Miss Makepeace said abruptly, strain flattening her vowels more than usual. "Would you tell me what the procedure is?"

"They just ask you to tell them exactly what happened last night," said Darina, studying the woman opposite her. The countrywoman was sitting upright, her shoulders braced back, straining against the same crimplene dress she'd worn the previous night. The plain, round face was weatherbeaten, a spray of white lines radiating out from each eye. Darina had a picture of Miss Makepeace wrinkling her eyes against the sun and the wind. Now, though, they were filled with concern.

"And what if you aren't sure exactly what happened?"

Something deep inside Darina went very still.

"What do you mean, Miss Makepeace?"

"It was that business with the dog."

Darina found herself relaxing. "It was rather confusing, wasn't it? I hadn't realised you saw anything, I thought you must have been asleep."

"I was on my way to the bathroom. I couldn't sleep. I have some pills but they make me feel a little odd the morning after and I wanted to be fully alert for the papers today. But finally I thought I would have to take half a one and went for some fresh water. I could see the last flight of stairs from over the balustrade. I suppose I should have gone down but I was reluctant to get involved, I was wrestling with my own problem and I didn't know it would be so important. On the other hand, it may not be important at all. Well, the Lord will deal with my weakness, for weakness it was."

Darina blinked but Miss Makepeace seemed quite serious. "Would you like to tell me what it was you saw? Perhaps I could help you sort it out?"

Miss Makepeace opened her mouth, then closed it again. The brown eyes searched Darina's grey ones, then she sighed and shook her head. "It's probably not at all important. And if it is, I don't think I should be mentioning it to anyone but the police."

It was infuriating but she was obviously not going to say anything more and Darina did not like to press her, she seemed worried enough. "Well, all you have to do is go through what you saw step by step. Just answer the questions the police will ask, there is no need to be worried." Darina hoped they would take her gently through the events. If the young sergeant was allowed to do the questioning, she thought Miss Makepeace would be all right. Then she heard his voice along the corridor:

"Mr. Childe, the inspector would be grateful if he could have a few words with you, please."

They'd finished with Nicholas, then. And now another innocent was being led to the slaughter. Surely they couldn't have dug up a motive for Charles to have killed her cousin?

That reminded her. Unlikely a murderer though Miss Makepeace appeared, last night had revealed a very strong motive for hating Digby.

"I have something to confess to you, Miss Makepeace. I'm afraid I unwittingly overheard your conversation with Digby Cary in the refectory after dinner last night."

The strong fingers scratched at the moquette covering the armchair. "I thought you had heard something, I saw you come round the screen, but I couldn't stay, I was too upset."

"Did Digby really base his book entirely on your work?"

The pebble glasses flashed. "There's no doubt about it, Miss Lisle. It's all there, all my facts, details, references. He just rewrote it all, placing the developments in context, drawing conclusions I would never have been able to make. His background knowledge is, was, much wider than mine and his mind less pedestrian. His book is witty and delightful to read. But the basic facts are all mine." Miss

Makepeace was prosaic, acknowledging the limits of her abilities with
a wry acceptance.

Darina eyed her sceptically. "How did you get started on such a
time-consuming enterprise?"

The tense figure relaxed slightly. "You're right to ask that, my
dear, it does sound an unlikely enterprise, doesn't it? I think my
parents would have been rather shocked. They didn't hold with edu-
cation for girls. They were yeoman farmers. We've lived in the same
Somerset farmhouse for over three hundred years. It nearly broke
their hearts there was no son to carry on, just my sister and me. It's
not very large, small dairy herd, some goats and chickens and a little
arable. Mary and I said we'd manage things. I'd like to have stayed on
at school, sat A levels, but they didn't see the sense in that, not if I
was going to work on the farm. So I left. And I enjoyed it. Hard work
has never bothered us, we were both of us strong. When my father
died, a year after mother, we found a man to help and it was a good
life."

"Neither of you married?"

Something like a twinkle appeared in Miss Makepeace's eye. "We
didn't want for suitors, not with that nice little farm. But somehow
neither Mary nor I found a man we could fancy. We enjoyed reading
and talking, you see, we'd discuss any amount of matters in the
evenings over our books and somehow none of the chaps seemed
able to join in. Their conversation was limited to drenches and reme-
dies for mastitis. All important matters in their place, but not very
stimulating.

"But you were asking how I got started on my research. Well, we
had a new vicar and he started a weekly discussion group on religious
questions. Most interesting, I enjoyed it so much. Then he suggested
I enrolled in the new Open University. I wanted Mary to join as well
only she said she preferred reading anything she wanted and she
didn't like the thought of having to write TMAs—those were the
essays we had to send in—and take exams. But I loved it." The soft
voice grew dreamy and matter-of-fact; Miss Makepeace glowed like a
girl in love.

"I thought I'd concentrate on literature but it was history that I
found more fascinating and, to tell the truth, all that dissection of
books we had to do in the foundation course put me right off En-

glish. So I took history courses, all the way up to the fourth-level one on historiography." Unashamed pride rang in her voice. "At the end I wanted to do some research of my own. I discussed it with my tutor. He asked me what really interested me and I told him about the family cookery book. We have a lovely, handwritten recipe book, brought into the family by an eighteenth-century bride—she must have been a catch for a Makepeace. I thought it would be nice to find out more about the sort of food and cooking that those old recipes represented. And compare them with those of other centuries. In many ways the cooking was so different from what we do today and yet in other ways there were so many similarities.

"So I started on that and the pastry side just seemed to take over. It tied in so many developments in techniques and cooking equipment and the way meals evolved."

"There's no chance Digby's research followed the same lines as yours, that you merely both went to the same sources?"

"Oh, Miss Lisle, don't you think I hadn't thought of that? When I first read the book, I was caught in two minds. One part of me knew what he must have done, but the other said what you have just suggested. So I went through it most carefully and so many little things told me he must have based it on my work. There's a recipe for an almond tart. Well, there are so many, many recipes for almond tarts in the seventeenth and eighteenth centuries. He could have chosen any of them. But the one he included is word for word the one I used, which was taken from that family manuscript book. I have never found it in any published work in exactly that form. But I didn't identify it as such and Mr. Cary may well have thought it was from some printed source.

"Then there's his account of flour milling. He describes the eighteenth-century milling machine with the linen sleeve exactly as I did but infers it is English. It's not, it's German. My sister and I were on a holiday in the Black Forest and I saw it there. I just failed to make that clear in my manuscript. It was a last-minute addition." Anxiety coloured Miss Makepeace's voice that her scholarship might be found lacking.

"Did you really not keep a copy of it?"

"It was as much as I could do to type one copy, I couldn't cope with carbons. It's an ancient machine, I found it at a local jumble sale, and I'm no typist. That manuscript was a mess. If Mr. Cary had said it was any good, I was planning to use what little savings I had to get it professionally typed." The firm mouth thinned, the lips, untouched by artificial aids, lost their natural colour. "It never occurred to me there was any need to keep a copy. I've never had anything lost in the post and I thought Mr. Cary an honourable man." Darina flinched at the note in her voice. "I was so grateful to him for offering to give me an opinion on the work. I'd spent so many years on it and reached the stage where I really had to have an authoritative assessment of its worth."

"But why on earth didn't you get in touch with him when you didn't hear anything?"

"At first I was so relieved not to have it back and be told it was no good; you see, every post I expected it to arrive with a polite note encouraging me to keep on being 'a busy little bee'—I knew exactly what that would mean." Deep scorn filled her voice. "Then Mary got ill. She'd always been overweight and had trouble with her stomach. Doctor said she had water on it, such a strange thing, don't you think? What harm can water do? But they said an operation was necessary and she'd have to diet. Poor thing, she found it truly difficult. I was so involved with keeping her to it, preparing special food, running the farm and trying to keep her cheerful, I really forgot about the book." Miss Makepeace blinked very hard, the muscles of her face tightening in a painful way. "When they told me she'd never come round after the operation, I couldn't believe it. We were so close, I was sure I'd have known if she was that ill. It was such a shock."

Darina got up and refilled their glasses. She brought them back and Miss Makepeace drank a little. When she spoke again, her voice was back to its matter-of-fact tone.

"Then I found things were in a pretty state. We hadn't been able to make any repairs to the house for years and suddenly everything seemed to fall apart. The roof started letting in water like a sieve. The window frames were so rotten I could hardly open one for fear it would fall out and then there was a small fire caused by faulty wiring. It all needed replacing. And there was no money. The farm was already mortgaged and if Mary hadn't had a small insurance policy, I don't know how I could have paid for her funeral.

"I discussed it all with the vicar. He knows nothing about finance but he put me in touch with another of his parishioners, who was most helpful. The only way out, he said, was to sell up. I wouldn't hear of it at first: sell my family's home for over three hundred years? They'd never forgive me, I said. Finally we worked out that, even with the price of farmland these days, if I sold most of the land and kept the house, I'd raise enough to do the repairs and produce a tiny income. I could keep a goat, a few sheep and chickens and raise my vegetables. I'd be almost self-sufficient. But I wouldn't be able to go abroad or afford much travelling, and I've got so used to my little trips visiting libraries and record offices digging out old manuscripts and rare cookery books; Mary was so good about my going off every now and then, said it was much better to spend any spare cash on that rather than silly old paint. It was she who insisted on the Black Forest holiday when we got some unexpected subsidy money." Miss Makepeace rubbed at her eyes briefly.

"Then I remembered my book and I thought if Mr. Cary had had time to read it, he might be able to tell me if a publisher could be interested in it. But before I could write to him, I found his book in our local shop. It was"—Miss Makepeace paused, unable to find the right word—"a shock." The word was anti-climactic but her tone revealed the depths of the experience.

She finished her second glass of wine then sat looking down at the carpet for a little while. Finally she raised her eyes and Darina was shaken by the raw pain shining through the thick lenses. "I find I cannot forgive him his action, Miss Lisle, my heart is full of vile thoughts. I am even glad"—the soft voice sank to a whisper—"that he is dead."

"It's only natural—" started Darina but Miss Makepeace hardly seemed to hear her.

"Revenge cannot be mine, it's the Lord's. 'I will repay,' he said. I kept thinking of that this morning when I heard the news. For a moment I felt responsible, it was almost as though I had called his death upon him."

Darina couldn't think of anything to say. She put her hand over Miss Makepeace's rough brown one and held it for a moment. Then an idea occurred to her. "Have you thought that it might be possible to do something about the book?"

Miss Makepeace's eyes swam slowly into focus. "What do you mean?"

"If you can write down all the pieces of evidence that might prove your case, like the almond tart recipe and the milling machine, and gather up any notes you still have, it might be possible to approach Digby's publishers."

Miss Makepeace's mouth opened, then closed, a dim light starting to glow in her eyes. "Do you really think so?" A deep sigh shook her body, then she said, "Do you think my manuscript might possibly still be in his house?"

That thought had not occurred to Darina. Would Digby have kept such an incriminating piece of evidence? If he thought there was no chance of anyone searching for it, why not? It probably contained references he might need.

"Well, and how are we ladies this evening?" Nicholas broke into their conversation. He had entered the bar with Linda. They had the relaxed, sleek look of cats who have indulged in enjoyable exercise. Linda had changed into a very short, red and black silk dress. It suited her polished looks to perfection. She carried a dramatic black and gold scarf and, looking at Linda's almost naked back, Darina thought she might need it, as the abbey central heating had not yet been turned on for the winter and the refectory was a chilly place.

Nicholas was in the suit he'd worn the night before, with a pink shirt and dark tie. Without asking Linda for her preference, he poured out two glasses of whisky, added water then brought over the wine bottle and refilled Darina and Miss Makepeace's glasses.

"How did your interview go?" asked Darina.

A little of his relaxation disappeared. "They kept coming back to what it was I wanted to see Digby about. When I said it was only some details of today's programme, they obviously didn't believe me. They kept on asking if I hadn't gone to see him when I left the bar last night. Asked if we hadn't quarrelled over the society. They wouldn't leave it alone. Anyone would think I'd done the murder."

"And did you?" Gray had entered the bar unobserved. He, too, had changed and his normally exuberant hair was sleeked to his skull as though he'd stood under a shower for some considerable time. He stood quietly in the doorway and looked steadily at Nicholas.

"My dear fellow," the professor blustered, "what possible motive could I have had for murdering poor Digby?"

Gray walked over to the bar and helped himself to a whisky and soda. "Jealousy, Professor. He challenged your authority, you never have been able to stand that, have you?"

To Darina's intense interest, Nicholas whitened, his nose looking suddenly pinched and sharp. He drew in a shallow breath, seemed about to speak, changed his mind, then started again. "I don't know what you are talking about, Wyndham, Digby and I have always worked closely together."

"I have been meaning to ask how the two of you got together." For once Linda had made a tactful move and Darina could have cursed her. How could her usually well-honed instinct for the good story desert her now? How close were she and Nicholas becoming?

Turning his back on Gray, Nicholas sank into a chair beside the producer and grasped at the opportunity to deflect the discussion into a new path. "I had uncovered some mediaeval privies and we were going to analyse the contents. One of the nationals got hold of the story and printed it in a typically facetious way, 'Not a turd unturned,' 'The droppings of history,' you can imagine the sort of thing. So it was a refreshing change to have Digby Cary arriving with a serious interest in the analysis results and prepared to appreciate just what such a find could mean."

"Do you mean," asked Darina, her interest caught despite her desire to have had Gray's interesting attack developed, "you could actually find out what people of that time had been eating?"

"Exactly," Nicholas beamed at her. "Our investigation threw new light on the dietary habits of fourteenth-century man. Digby was enormously excited. We had several fruitful meetings, then I asked him round for a meal. I've always had a deep interest in the history of food and, without knowing much about cookery, I spent quite a bit of time experimenting with old recipes. I think," Nicholas chuckled, "old Digby was quite astonished to get an authentic John Knott recipe from his 1726 *Dictionary of Cooking.*

"Of course, he had to ask me back. Went right over the top with a full-blown olio that would have fed a small army. Joints of beef and tongue, sausage from Bologna, chunks of mutton, pork, venison and bacon and another pot with a small turkey, a capon, pheasant, duck, partridge and, if my memory serves me right, even a quail." Nicholas's eyes glowed with the memory. For once, envy of Digby seemed to have been forgotten in the enchantment of food.

"Then there was a third pot with artichoke bottoms, chestnuts, cauliflower and broccoli in white wine and stock. He took me into the kitchen to watch him serve it up and garnish it with hard-boiled egg yolks, pistachio nuts, slices of beetroot and lemon, finally dribbling melted butter over all."

There was a little silence as Nicholas finished his description. Linda looked quite faint.

"It tasted incredible, we lingered over it the entire afternoon."

"We're having a version of that for lunch tomorrow," said Darina.

A touch of peevishness returned to Nicholas. "No doubt Digby thought he could work in a good reference to the start of the society that would go down well with the media!" He pressed Linda's hand in mute apology. "Because that was how we got started. One or other of us would cook an historical meal every few months or so and ask others to join us. My friends were mostly academics and Digby's were from the food world. They seemed to get on well and the idea for the society arose quite naturally." He turned and gave Linda a big smile, his chipmunk face at its most attractive.

How much more confident he seemed now than yesterday, thought Darina. Was it the obvious success he was having with Linda, or was it because Digby was no longer there to overshadow him?

"Don't you all look cosy!" Rita entered the bar, a loose dress of flowered chiffon floating round her. "I'm so glad to see you've all dressed up, too. I wondered if it wouldn't be a mark of disrespect, then thought that Digby would have liked us to look good." Her copper hair sprang around her head in a fiery aureole, crackling with life.

Gray waved the whisky bottle at her in an unspoken invitation. She nodded gratefully, "Thank you, that would be just great, I find a day doing nothing is totally exhausting. This waiting around is a great strain. How much longer is it to go on, does anyone know?"

"Until they find the murderer, I suppose." Gray brought over her drink and sat himself in a chair beside her.

"I assume they'll have finished interviewing us all by tomorrow morning and then we'll be able to get home," Nicholas said.

"You think they're going to find the murderer that easily, do you?"

Nicholas flushed at the jeering note in Gray's voice. "They will, of course, have more ground to cover, I don't suppose they'll be able to wrap up their investigation—isn't that the jargon?—that quickly. There must be other people they need to talk to."

"You're not deluding yourself one of us isn't the murderer?" Gray was scornful.

"One of us the murderer? Saints alive, what about all the other symposiasts?" Strain showed in Rita's face despite the skilfully applied make-up; dark circles ringed the sea-green eyes and pallor accentuated the freckles running across her nose.

"Why do you think they were so summarily chased off the premises?" Gray got up from his chair and walked across to the empty fireplace, then stood facing them. "Use your brains. The murderer must have known where to find Digby Cary last night. There was only us and Charles Childe in the bar when Darina brought in the message. Ergo, it was one of us who killed him."

"But couldn't anyone have found him in that room?" persisted Rita.

"The chances of a symposiast wandering through the refectory, down past the kitchen, along that corridor and locating the housekeeper's room on the off-chance of finding Digby are about as remote as Bracken coming top in an obedience class. No, if anyone had wanted Digby, the first place they would have looked would have been the bar, then they would have asked Nicholas. Did anyone ask for him last night, Professor?" Gray invested the title with an ironic twist that made Nicholas raise his head sharply. Then he shook it.

"No, no one."

"But surely," protested Rita, "if someone had wanted to find Digby in order to kill him, they'd hardly have gone around advertising the fact."

"If it was a premeditated murder, I'd agree with you. But don't you think it sounds much more as if it was a spur of the moment crime?" He turned to Darina. "You said that there was a display of kitchen knives in that room, didn't you?" She nodded. "And where were they?"

"On a table in the middle of the room."

Gray turned back to the others. "There you are, all too easy to pick one up. The murderer might not have had murder on his mind at all until Digby drove him, or her, just that bit too far. Blind with rage, they snatched up one of the knives and stuck it in him." He made a rather wild lunge with his hand that made Rita jerk back in her chair. Her face grew even paler. Linda flinched but Miss Makepeace maintained the composure with which she had listened to everything that had been said since Nicholas entered the bar.

Darina saw a chance to get in one of the questions that had been worrying her. "Nicholas, did Digby advertise the fact he was going to sell the knives?"

"Not as far as I know. And I knew nothing," he added bitterly. "Digby didn't see fit to tell even me. If he had mentioned he was setting up a shop, I could have brought in some of my books, God knows we all need sales."

There was silence. The implications of the murder investigation seemed to have brought the gathering to the point where a Trappist monk would have seemed talkative.

Darina looked at her watch. "It's time I went to check on the meal," she said as brightly as she could manage. "I think Charles Childe is being interviewed at the moment, should we wait for him? And should I ask the inspector if he and the sergeant want to eat with us?"

Nicholas thought for a moment, then sighed. "I suppose we should at least ask," he said reluctantly, "though I can't think it will make for a pleasant meal. But only if they've finished with Mr. Childe. I don't think we should wait any longer."

But at that moment Charles Childe exploded into the bar.

"You'll never guess what that bastard did!" The words were flung into the air like grape-shot. He went straight to the bar, poured himself a large gin, added a dash of Angostura bitters and drank deeply. As he turned towards the waiting faces, a palpable change came over him. The wildness calmed and the actor took control, leaning back against the bar, prepared to launch into his performance.

"Digby Cary," he said, carefully controlling his obvious anger, "saw fit to crucify my restaurant."

"Crucify your restaurant?" repeated Rita. "How?"

"Those nit-picking policemen have found his last restaurant column. You remember how I was afraid Digby had died before he could write my restaurant up? Well, I'd have preferred him to have died before writing *this* column." He gave a little toss of his head and took another slug of drink.

"What did he say?" Linda was all agog.

"Only that there was no more pretentious restaurant in London, that the food lacked any understanding of basic cookery principles and sacrificed flavour for effect. That my food should have a right to sue for the crimes committed on it. Oh, there was more if I could but remember it. Mercifully, perhaps, I can't." He put down his drink and with a trembling hand brushed the fair hair back from his anguished face.

"Will it be published?" asked Linda with eager interest.

Charles picked up his drink again and took another deep swig. "What the police found is the carbon copy. Dated yesterday. The sixty-four thousand dollar question, darling, the one that wins the safari holiday *and* the cuddly toy, is where has the original gone?"

"If it is the one he was writing last night," said Darina slowly, "I saw him stapling it together before dinner. He said it had to catch this morning's mail."

"Could he have posted it last night? And, if so, could it be published posthumously?" Charles looked deeply worried but without pausing for an answer, he continued, "Totally ignoring the fact I knew nothing of this travesty of an article, the police seemed to think it could have given me a motive for murder! Then, when I told them I went down last night to ask Digby if he'd managed to write up my restaurant, only to find that he was having a ding-dong of an argument with a female with the most *charming* of Irish accents, they decided to ask you, Rita darling, if you'd go and have a little talk with them instead."

FIFTEEN

All eyes swivelled to Rita. She shrank back into the chair, her face now paper white. For a moment she looked as though she was about to deny the story. Then she drew a deep breath. "Sure 'tis the little darling you are, Charles. Do you think they're going to arrest me?"

"We should just like a few words with you, Ms. Moore, if you please." Sergeant Pigram stood quietly in the doorway looking at each of them with interest.

Darina seized her chance. "How long will you be, Sergeant? We should like to serve dinner shortly and we wondered if you and the inspector would be joining us?"

He seemed taken aback at this offer of hospitality. "Inspector Grant will have to make the decision on that." He stood aside to allow Darina to lead the way out of the room, then ushered Rita after her.

Inspector Grant was oblivious to the charms of dinner. "We are trying to get through the interviews before tomorrow afternoon," he said, motioning a nervous Rita to the chair in front of the writing desk. "I'm afraid you will have to go ahead without Ms. Moore. We won't keep her longer than we have to." He stretched his mouth in a grimace that could just be called a smile. "We wouldn't refuse a plate of left-overs when our interview with her has finished, though—we seem to have been too busy for lunch."

Dinner was not a merry meal. Charles Childe harped on Digby's review. "It was malicious and unwarranted. My food is delicious, everyone says so. It's all because he was jealous over my success in that television series. He'd expected to dominate it, make a fool out of me, and I precious nearly turned the tables on him. I know he made sure a regular column writing about food didn't come my way."

"Where would that have been?" asked Linda, her scepticism plain.

Charles looked down at his plate, pushed the fat oysters and chicken livers around with his fork and mentioned one of the popular dailies. "I did a sort of food diary for them for a few weeks when the second series started. Initially they said it would run regularly but it was stopped when the television series ended and someone told me Digby had had a word with the editor." He sounded sulky and reluctant to give out details.

"If your column was any good, it is very unlikely Digby could have killed it." Linda spoke with calm authority.

Charles looked as though he might burst into tears.

"What a terrible weekend it's been for you," said Darina hurriedly. "First you're savaged by a dog and have to wear your arm in a sling, then you learn Digby wrote a bad review of your restaurant."

"You haven't mentioned the worst thing of all," said Charles archly. "My jacket," he added, "my beautiful Jean-Paul Gaultier jacket. Quite ruined, darling, no cleaner will be able to remove all that blood."

Charles's left hand still reposed in its sling. The bandage covered most of the hand, so that only the top halves of the fingers were free. Darina looked at it. "How long before you will be able to cook with that?" she asked. "And who's doing the cooking for you this weekend?"

"I have an assistant chef, in fact he does more than I do, really. I'm so often needed to help the ambience out front." Charles brightened as he talked of his venture. "He's a dear friend from years ago, wrote to me after the television series started, said he'd been working in a restaurant and why didn't we start one together. And then my aunt died and left me a little property; in darkest Tooting, but the most amazing people are *desperate* for nice little houses in Tooting these days. It made such a good sale and Shane said, why not put the leavings of the tax sharks toward a restaurant in Wandsworth? Such a difficulty getting a mortgage for the extra and all the conversion costs, my dears; you wouldn't believe how *vicious* some of these financial people can be.

"But we eventually found such a lovely chap, *muy simpático*, he's a dear friend now, comes into the restaurant all the time. Well, of course, we look after him, got to, haven't you?" Charles rambled on.

Nobody wanted to listen, nobody could stem the flow. Finally the need to eat his meal broke his remorseless recitation.

"Most interesting," said Nicholas hastily. "Darina, dear, why don't you tell us a little about the food you have prepared for us tonight?"

Darina tried to make some interesting comments but it was Miss Makepeace who provided a diverting topic of conversation.

"I was most interested in the title of the paper Mr. Cary was supposed to have delivered," she ventured. "What was it exactly? 'The Public versus the Private Cook in the Seventeenth and Eighteenth Centuries—Which were the True Recorders of the English Taste?' Something like that, anyway. Do you know, Professor, what it was to have contained?"

Nicholas's nose wrinkled slightly as if in response to food that was less than fresh. "Ah, yes, Digby had this idea one could find the genuine English taste in the private recipe collections, such as those of Kenelm Digby, Rebecca Price and Elizabeth Raper, rather than in the formal cookery books by chefs like Robert May, Charles Carter or Patrick Lamb."

"An interesting idea," pronounced Miss Makepeace, polishing off her oysters.

"Digby's theory was that the formal recipe books offered food for display. It reflected status rather than a free consumer choice, whereas the private cookery collections celebrated the food the English, particularly the country squire, actually preferred to eat. He said that outside court circles, entertaining in that period lacked the element of fashion and snobbishness that entered in the nineteenth century and eventually, he believed, led to the downfall of English cooking. His paper was to expand on this and draw comparisons between various books and collections."

"I don't suppose you could have agreed with the theory," Gray suggested with a malicious smile.

Nicholas frowned in a detached way. "I discussed it slightly with Digby. Conspicuous consumption has always been associated with wealth, and entertaining has been used as a way of displaying status since time immemorial. I think the idea of the eighteenth-century squire ignoring any such influence is a trifle naïve. Pepys's diary, for instance, displays his enjoyment of showing off his increasing wealth through entertaining, and other examples can be cited. On the other hand," he added judiciously, "Parson Woodforde just enjoyed good food."

"But there you are comparing a townie with a country cleric," protested Darina.

Nicholas was unperturbed. "Sir Kenelm Digby was a highly sophisticated cosmopolitan and he is the compiler of one of our chairman's private cookery collections. But it's dangerous to speculate on odd examples. I would need to examine a good deal more evidence than Digby seemed likely to offer before venturing an opinion."

"Hedging your bets, Professor?" Gray sounded jovial now.

"I have no reluctance to publish theories in respected journals for consideration by my peers, after my research has been completed. *My* academic standing is well recognized." Nicholas sounded as pointed as a trussing needle and Gray lost his good humour. Colour mounted under his beard as he stared at the professor, and he said no more.

"I wonder if future ages will judge our eating habits by studying *Gourmet* and *Taste* magazines?" said Linda, breaking the uneasy silence that had developed. "Neither gives much space to vegetarian eating, a movement gaining increasing popularity." She looked down at the tomato and basil salad Darina had prepared for her.

"Surely," interposed the cook, "those magazines are leading fashion, not producing what the average housewife wants to set before her family. They would have to be taken together with magazines offering broader appeal. I suppose that's basically what Digby was getting at." She got up to clear the plates and fetch the next course.

Bringing in steaming dishes of food, she reflected that Digby's spirit had really belonged in the eighteenth rather than the twentieth century. Its strong flavours, quick appreciation of new ingredients, robust enjoyment of both quality and quantity and no-holds-barred candid commenting on every aspect of life would have suited him down to the ground.

She put dishes of chicken and pigeon on the table and gave Linda a courgette timbale. The producer accepted it without comment.

Charles had no such reservations.

"I have to say you are a fantastic cook," he mumbled with his mouth full of chicken. "Such a wonderful idea, serving half of the bird casseroled and half grilled. And marvellous flavour. How's it done?"

"Marinated in wine and vinegar with various flavourings. It's one of Charles Carter's recipes," explained Darina. Charles looked blank. "He was chef to various nobility and published an extremely good cookery book in 1730."

"Can you take just any of these old recipes and cook them?"

Darina smiled. "It's not quite that simple, there are very few quantities given and the method is frequently sketchy. Sometimes it takes quite a lot of experimenting to get a satisfactory dish. And some of the ingredients are difficult to get hold of. I had a struggle to find the cockscombs."

"The what?"

"What did you think those little red things were?" It was symptomatic of everyone's preoccupation with other matters that no one had commented on these.

Charles lifted the little comb to his mouth gingerly. "Gristly!" he commented after trying it.

"They're an old delicacy that has recently been taken up again by the French. Try a pigeon in lettuce—this is another recipe from Carter, in fact the whole meal is from his book." She placed one of the small birds on his plate, sent the dish up the table, then took the breast off the bone for him.

Charles chewed enthusiastically. "Is it possible to get a copy of this book?"

Darina nodded. "Prospect Books recently published a facsimile edition."

"I've just got to try some of these old recipes in the restaurant, I'm sure we could be on to a winner and bring the press along. But experimenting with recipes sounds too frightening."

"It's not really, you just employ basic cookery principles and then use your own judgement. Take the carrot pudding that's coming next. The actual recipe calls for ten egg yolks plus the whites of five to half a pint of cream. Try that with today's eggs and you'd get a hopelessly solid concoction. Eggs at that time were a good deal smaller than ours, and so was the pint, which was the same as the American is today, sixteen fluid ounces instead of twenty. It's quite easy to see that the recipe is based on a custard mixture. Well, you

know the standard quantities for a custard"—Charles looked quite
bewildered—"three large egg yolks to half a pint of cream, or two
whole eggs and two egg yolks if you want a firmer set."

Charles Childe's chatter for once was mercifully stilled, and he
looked fascinated. "I didn't know any of that," he said.

"Whites set firmer, yolks give a more creamy result. Anyway, that
gives you your proportions for the cream and eggs, once you take
into account the amount of Madeira wine you're adding instead of
sack—the quantity isn't specified so it's up to you. As is the amount
of grated biscuit and the sugar and candied peel. There's quite a lot
of personal taste involved."

Charles was looking alarmed by now. "Perhaps we should employ
you as a consultant"—he shot a sly look at her—"I mean, your food
is so marvellous. That feast you produced for us last night. The
spiced beef could become a standard item, we could do things with it
for starters, or use it for a lunchtime cold table. Then those buttered
oranges looked spectacular and tasted gorgeous. And your touch
with pastry, just sensational, the complicated pattern on that large
tart was so attractive and as for that pie of stuffed birds, it was out of
this world. Can you give me recipes or do you charge for things like
that? We're a little strapped for cash at the moment but whatever it
costs, I must have them."

Charles continued to rattle on. Darina thought the wine he had
been freely drinking on top of the gin he had had beforehand must
have gone slightly to his head. Or perhaps it was the relief of having
escaped, at least for the present, from the police interrogation. She
remembered how unnerving her own interview had been. How was
Rita standing up to hers, she wondered.

Darina was not the only one. Linda looked at her watch. "Rita's
been a long time," she said, a note almost of satisfaction in her voice.

"Is the length of time in an interview a measure of guilt?" asked
Gray. "How long were you in there, Professor?" There was challenge
in his voice.

"About fifty minutes," said Nicholas briefly, undecided whether
this was a matter for pride or concern. "And how about you?" He
returned the challenge.

"Just over an hour." Gray tried to sound unconcerned. "Give those
two a pile of stones and the hospital service would never want for

blood. They took me through the details of last night's events so many times I thought they'd bring Bracken in for corroboration. When they finally let me go, it was with the comforting thought they might need to speak to me again."

"It's such a shattering experience, I've known nothing like it since the first of those TV programmes, the way they sit there and fire questions at you. I needed that drink, I can tell you." Charles seemed to have recovered from his shock at hearing Digby's last restaurant review and was now enjoying the drama of the occasion.

Miss Makepeace looked quite ill. She pushed away a plate of half-eaten food, closed her notebook and drank some of the wine.

Darina got up and started clearing away. The tensions around the table were almost tangible.

The puddings helped to provide a slight lightening of the atmosphere.

"Had the symposium been able to continue, there would have been more dishes," said Nicholas, "and we would have mixed the sweet and the savoury, as we did last night. It's quite anachronistic to serve them segregated in this way."

"Service à la Russe," said Miss Makepeace unexpectedly.

Heads swung towards her end of the table. "That's what this type of service was called when it was introduced in the middle of the nineteenth century." She warmed to her subject, a little colour coming back into her face. "In Russia and Scandinavia they had the habit of serving each dish individually instead of arranging several on the table at the same time. Gradually the practice spread over here. By the end of the nineteenth century, with the increasing formality of entertaining, it had taken over completely." She tried the carrot pudding then turned to Darina. "Forgive me, Miss Lisle, but I think you have used altogether too much sugar. With dishes such as this, it was used more as a seasoning than a sweetener. They were not treated as dessert dishes as we understand them."

Nicholas pounced on the opportunity to revive the company's interest in the food but it proved heavy going and the party quite quickly rose from the table to take coffee in the bar.

After arranging with Frances for the coffee, Darina turned her attention to the abandoned dishes on the table. As she placed uneaten raspberry creams on a tray, Rita entered, pale but composed.

"Darina, darling, would there be a morsel of food for an exhausted suspect?"

"Sit here, have some wine and I'll just put your Attlets under the grill."

A few minutes later she placed the loaded skewers in front of Rita and sent Frances off with a tray of food for the inspector and sergeant, thankful that the other police seemed to have disappeared from the abbey.

"Have you time to sit with me?" asked Rita. "I hate eating alone, I have to do it so often."

"I'll take out the last of the dirty dishes so the kitchen can deal with them, then I'll be delighted to."

Darina carried a loaded tray into the kitchen, returning with Rita's chicken and pigeons.

"Those oysters were good, what did you say they were called?"

"Attlets."

"And what sort of name would that be?"

Darina sat herself opposite the Irish woman and poured wine for them both. "I've discovered when in doubt over a word in old recipes, look to French. Larousse describes 'attlets' as silver skewers." She watched Rita help herself to a generous portion of the chicken, allowed her to eat for a few minutes, then asked tentatively, "Did you really have an argument with Digby last night?"

Rita made a slight face. "After my experience with the inspector, I cannot tell a lie. When Nicholas didn't seem anxious to go and talk with the great man last night, it seemed an ideal opportunity for me to tackle him about help for my research. So down I came and it would not be overstating the case to say he was not in a receptive mood. One word led to another and we were at it like cats and dogs. But finally we arrived at agreement and there seemed little point mentioning it this morning when I knew I left him alive and well. I hadn't realised that little fairy was listening outside the door."

"But you could have been the last to see him alive," interjected Darina, "apart, that is, from . . ." Her voice tailed away.

Rita nodded. "Apart from the murderer. Unless, of course, I was the murderer. It was a stupid thing to do, I realise that now, I should have said immediately that I'd been with him."

"How soon after I left the bar did you go down?"

"Gray announced he was going to take that benighted animal of his for a walk. I went upstairs and collected my notes on the new book, just in case Digby wanted to discuss them. Gray was disappearing out of the front door as I came down again and I went straight through this room and down to Digby's office."

"How long were you with Digby?"

Rita groaned. "And that's the question the police asked. I wasn't looking at clocks and I was so wrought up anyway Father Time could have moved hands several times around without my noticing but, realistically, after going through what I could remember of what we'd both said, and certain phrases are etched into my brain, we concluded it must have been no more than about twelve minutes. Whoever would have thought twelve minutes could last so long."

"What did you argue about?"

Before Rita could reply, Linda came into the refectory, neat and composed as always. She headed for the place where she had been sitting. "I had a wrap, did I leave it in here?"

"Ah, Miss Linda Stainmore!" There was acid under the Irish charm of Rita's voice. "Don't leave," she added as the producer picked up the insubstantial fabric from under the table and turned to go, "there's something I want to ask you."

Linda shrugged her shoulders and stood at the end of the table, an exotic insect poised for an instant before darting off to a more interesting plant.

Rita indicated a place beside Darina. "Will you sit yourself down, this could take some time."

Linda looked at her steadily for a moment, then shrugged her narrow shoulders and took a seat.

Rita buttered a piece of roll, ate it, then looked across at her. "How long was it before Digby broke up with you?"

A wave of bright red washed over Linda's face as she sat rigidly staring across the table at Rita.

"What do you mean?" she said at last.

"My dear, no need to act injured innocence. I was your predecessor. I knew exactly when rehearsals for his new TV show had turned into something altogether more interesting. And then I saw you in a restaurant, not very clever of Digby to have chosen such a dark corner for the two of you, far too obvious."

"I think I should go and check things in the kitchen." Darina got up, good manners winning over a strong desire to stay and see how this promising start developed.

Rita waved an impatient hand at her. "You stay right there, I'd prefer there to be a witness to this little scene, I don't want any misunderstandings later. Now, Miss Stainmore, why don't you relax a little and give us the truth."

Linda sat rigidly straight. "Dining with a man doesn't mean you're sleeping with him. Half the men in London would be sued for adultery if that was the case."

Rita sighed. "I never expected Digby to leave his wife, but, fool that I was, I didn't dream there were others. The stories that man could spin, a frigid wife he couldn't bear to hurt, no mention that she had the money. I was the only woman he'd ever really loved, the only woman he could share his deepest interests with and I believed him . . . It was fine so long as I was safely married to my husband, poor man, but then we divorced and Digby felt threatened." Rita pushed away her plate and reached for a raspberry cream. "I knew there was someone else and I didn't need to be much of a detective to find out it was you."

As Rita spoke, Linda gradually not so much relaxed as sagged. Confidence leaked away. The wash of colour retreated; against the black hair, her face took on the look of a clown. Her dress suddenly seemed garish. Gone was the polished professional, secure in her sophistication; instead there was a girl with rather ordinary looks in a fancy dress that didn't suit.

"So I repeat my question, how long did you have before Digby moved on to someone new?"

Linda attempted to pull herself together. "I don't think it's any of your business."

"And what is it you are so busy pointing your darling little TV cameras at if it's not a murder investigation? With me being treated as a prime suspect? I'll say it's my business.

"I'll tell you what I think. I think you came here intending to attract Digby into your little web once more. Don't think I didn't notice the looks you gave him and the flirtation with the poor professor. Don't think I didn't try that too at one time, for Digby always had the instincts of an alley cat; he'd drop you like a stale sardine if better fish appeared but let anyone else try to pick you up and he'd be there, claws out. But only for a time and that time was long past for us both." Linda was staring at Rita, held as fascinated as some small animal caught by headlights on a dark road.

"So, didn't you decide you'd have one more shot at him? Didn't you go down to that office after I'd left? And wouldn't he have been at his most scathing? After all, there was that charming actress he was preparing like a chicken for roasting, basting with his flattery till she was ready to fall off the bone—he'd have no more time for your advances than he had for my pleas for help. You would have got all upset. And angry. For hadn't you devoted some of the best years of your life to the darling man? And hadn't he kicked you where it hurt most? And wasn't there a nice sharp knife to hand?"

"No!" Linda shouted at the Irish woman.

Rita sat back looking at the trembling girl with satisfaction. "No?" she asked softly.

"No," repeated Linda in a slightly lower key. With a great effort she gathered herself together. "OK, you are right about Digby. I did think he loved me. To start with, it was only rehearsals, private rehearsals." Rita threw her a look of transcendent scorn. "That's all they were. I'd offered to help him develop his approach to camera, and I did. That was the series that really established Digby as a TV star. But we fell in love. And you're right about that, too, I did think he was serious. After all, I didn't have time for a casual affair. If you're to get on in the TV world, total dedication is necessary.

"It's not been easy for me"—Linda's hand trembled as she reached for a glass and poured herself some wine—"I've come up the hard way, without a degree, starting as a researcher. And we made a great team. I had all sorts of ideas for programme series and videos with Digby, we could have climbed together." She fell silent, looking at her dreams reflected in the glass of limpid gold. "When I got offered promotion to Bristol, I told Digby I was going to turn it down, go freelance and develop my ideas with him." Linda raised a ravaged face to Darina. "He told me it was all finished, that there wasn't anybody else but he felt it was unfair to me to continue when he would never be able to leave his wife. Of course I told him I didn't care about not being able to marry but then he said he'd signed an exclusive contract with a production company to do a series of cookery videos. So that had gone as well. Even then he made me believe he'd agreed for my sake, that it was so I wouldn't be tied to him in any way.

"All that was left for me to do was to take the Bristol job." She fell silent. Neither Darina nor Rita spoke.

"That was the end of it really. But when Digby came to Bristol, he would get in touch and we would have a meal—for old times' sake, he'd say." Linda's mouth twisted painfully. "Then his wife died. I thought he would come down, or at least ring, but I heard nothing until he contacted me a few weeks ago about this weekend. I was so delighted, I thought he wanted to get together again. I persuaded my controller to do a half-hour programme rather than a quick few minutes. Then I arrived and found Digby had no intention of anything more. He only wanted to use me, as he'd done before."

For a moment Darina thought Linda was going to burst into tears. The vivid dress had slipped off one shoulder and her lipstick was smudged where she'd drawn her hand across her mouth as she finished. But she blinked rapidly, straightened her back and looked across at Rita.

"And you were right about my initial contact with Nicholas. I did think it might make Digby jealous. But I really do like him now. I think he's marvellous. Such a mind, such learning, and actually wanting to talk to me." A childlike wonder filled her face and she spoke with a shy dignity that touched Darina.

Rita sighed. "So what you are saying is that you meekly accepted the fact that Digby had played you for a sucker and merely transferred your attentions to our resident academic. That not for a moment did you think of trying to use your charms to get Digby back?"

Linda flushed. "I might have but I didn't have the chance." Now tears did fill her eyes.

"Well, I hope you can manage a more convincing account for the police than you have for me." But Rita sounded doubtful. She looked tired, the fine skin was papery, the lines beside her mouth deeper and Darina realised she must be well into middle age.

Linda stood up and drew her shawl around her shoulders, not bothering how it looked, and hugged it across her flat front. "I don't care what you think, it's what happened. Now I'm going back to the bar," she said defiantly and left the room.

Rita turned to Darina. "Do you believe all that?"

"Do you really think she could be the murderer?"

"I knew only too well how murderous her feelings for Digby could be, so why not? He was alive when I left him."

"Why was Digby so reluctant to discuss your project? It sounds so unlike him, he always tried to keep on good terms with—" Darina hesitated for a moment, wondering how to put it.

"With his past mistresses, you mean?" Rita helped her out, her tone wry. "Yes, well, there was an unfortunate incident on a daytime television spot we shared just after he broke off with me. Not a production of Linda's, I hasten to add, it was in one of the northern studios. We were supposed to be putting over ideas with eggs, one of those quick ten-minute spots, live and in front of an audience. And on camera he dropped my soufflé. You never saw such a high riser. He wasn't even meant to touch it but, always so keen to stick a finger in every pie, he had to take it out of the oven. He'd been upset at my share of the programme, and was it my fault if the producer liked my ideas better than his? I swear he dropped it on purpose. One moment my lovely soufflé was rising higher than the Empire State and the next it was all over the studio floor!

"And didn't he try to look apologetic? Bent down to pick up the pieces. And everything he'd done to me all of a sudden rose up in my breast like overproved dough. I picked up a copper bowl filled with eggs and emptied it over his head. The mess was *wonderful*. And then he turned all dignified and made me look like a fishwife. That was the last programme anyone has asked me to do on television. Did you never hear about it?"

Darina shook her head. "It must have been whilst I was abroad for some months. It doesn't sound the sort of thing Digby would boast about. What a shame I missed it, I'd love to have seen him with egg on his face."

Rita giggled. "It was a sight that comforted me mightily in the months that followed. I still have it on video, I must show it to you

some day." Then the laughter fizzled out like bubbles from unconsumed champagne.

"It was the end of a somewhat promising career for me. Oh, I
suppose it'd been going downhill for some years. My television series
was too early, it was before cooking hit the big time. And my books
didn't have mass appeal. To tell you the truth, I was having a struggle to make ends meet after my marriage went down the drain. I'd
thought that programme with Digby might revive things for me.
Instead of which it seems to have been the end.

"And you have no idea how soul-destroying it is to have to suffer
constant rejection. Even worse is not having anything positive to tell
friends who ask what you're doing. Do you realise your identity be-
longs to your achievements? Doing nothing, you *are* nothing. And it
was all due to Digby." She rested her chin on her fists, her arms
propped up on the table, her eyes fixed on the far wall. Then she
brought her gaze back to Darina.

"Finally I found a publisher for a book. I'd been working on cooking in Irish country houses with a mixture of old and new recipes.
They're quite enthusiastic about it and have suggested I do the same
for English country houses. So I enrolled for this weekend. For information and because I thought Digby could help me out with some
contacts, might even be persuaded to prepare an introduction, for
old times' sake. His name on the cover would have helped sales
enormously.

"But when I knocked on his door yesterday evening I found he
hadn't forgotten the egg incident. Such a tiny thing beside what he
had done to me. And so I told him. What a shouting match!" A
wealth of satisfaction rang in Rita's voice. "I told him he was totally
selfish, that he used people, sucked them dry then threw them away
without a second thought. And he suddenly changed completely.
Told me he was sorry, he'd behaved like a heel and then he promised
to do everything he could to help me. Oh, the charm of the man!
The first time he'd ever apologised. I was prepared to forgive and
forget . . ." A reminiscent smile lit her face, then her expression
changed again. "The shock it was this morning to find he'd been
murdered."

The word hung in the air infecting the atmosphere like a virus.

Darina rose. "If you've finished, I must take the last of the dishes to the kitchen."

"Sure, I'll help you." Rita got up and together they cleared away the last plates.

SIXTEEN

When Darina and Rita entered the bar, Miss Makepeace was deep in a spirited discussion with Nicholas over the authenticity of the recipes in Anne Hughes's account of her life as a farmer's wife at the end of the eighteenth century. Linda, her polish back in place, was sitting beside them with her eyes fixed on Nicholas, the new man in her life.

Gray was sitting in a chair a little apart. He was reading, a pile of books by his side and an open notebook on a small table. He held a pencil and from time to time he made a note or marked a passage.

Charles was roaming round the room, peering at pictures on the wall, picking up a newspaper, glancing at the front page, tossing it down again and moving on to stand by the bar, his good hand beating a little tattoo on the counter. As Darina and Rita entered, his face lit up.

"At last! We heard our fair Irish maid was still at liberty. Come and have a brandy, I'm in the chair, it's a celebration for Digby's article on my restaurant not having been printed." His words were articulated very precisely.

"Oh," said Darina, "you've found out it hasn't gone then?"

Charles poured cognac into two glasses. "Well, no, but I don't think it could be printed now he's dead, do you?"

Darina thought it was more than likely that it would be but said nothing as she accepted the glass then watched him go round the others with the bottle, ignoring the half-hearted protests as he refilled their glasses. She sipped the excellent spirit, reflecting that care was going to be needed if they weren't all to be as under the influence as Charles appeared to be.

Rita joined Nicholas and Miss Makepeace, displaying a knowledge that seemed as wide as theirs. Darina sat in a chair to one side and

studied the Irish woman. How curious it was that both Linda and
Rita should have been Digby's mistresses. Two such different
women, yet neither of them had seemed at all concerned about
Digby's wife. Only their own feelings had worried them.

Could either of them have killed Digby? Rita's story had seemed
convincing. Yet she must be something of an actress to have appeared successfully in front of the television cameras. And no doubt
she'd had to think quickly and learn to dissemble to cover up disasters from time to time, disasters that had not been so all-engulfing as
that perpetrated by Digby. It was all too likely he had dropped that
soufflé deliberately. When his wishes were thwarted, he could be
very spiteful.

How cruel of him. No wonder Rita had reacted badly. So had they
both, locked into a situation where each looked a fool. But it had
been Rita who had suffered in the long term. Had she finally got her
revenge on Digby? Had he advanced on her in the housekeeper's
room, reliving the humiliation of the last time they'd met? Darina
suddenly saw a vision of her huge cousin in the grip of one of his
passions. He could be a frightening figure. Had Rita snatched up the
knife in self-defence, then somehow stabbed him?

No, Darina thought; she could imagine Rita lashing out in a com-
bination of fear and anger, even killing Digby. But she couldn't see
her leaving him dead or dying and then tending Charles's hand,
calmly drawing attention to Digby's absence and providing sympathy
for Nicholas. That called for a detachment, a cold-bloodedness she
didn't think the Irish woman possessed.

Now Linda was a different matter. Darina could imagine her filled
with bitterness and frustration snatching up the knife, wielding it to
deadly effect, and leaving the scene afterwards without turning a
hair. How bitter had she been over Digby's treatment of her?

Darina put aside the question of who killed Digby and turned to
how. If the knife had been snatched up in a moment of sudden
passion, surely the killer must have been standing near the table?
Would they have advanced with it? Wasn't it more likely Digby had
been advancing towards them? In which case, his body would have
fallen near the table. Darina tried to remember the position of the
body when she'd found it that morning but could not conjure up a
clear picture. She would have to check that. If the body were by the

desk, it would suggest murder rather than self-defence. And what would that prove? That the murderer was more likely to have been one of the men?

Nicholas's voice raised in outrage cut across her thoughts. "You don't know what you are saying, Miss Makepeace."

Darina looked up. The professor and Deborah Makepeace were facing each other like fighting turkey-cocks. Each was red with suppressed emotion, and the wisps of hair Nicholas so carefully combed across his pate were standing askew.

Miss Makepeace took a deep breath, looked as though she was about to say something but seemed temporarily to lose her power of speech. She took another breath and said steadily, enunciating each word with deliberate care, "I know exactly what I am talking about. Digby Cary stole my book and I can prove it, ask Miss Lisle."

Attention shifted to Darina.

"Well," demanded Nicholas, "what have you to say about this ridiculous statement?"

"From what Miss Makepeace has told me, I think her claim probably can be substantiated. There is also the possibility her original manuscript may be found in Digby's house." She gave brief details of Miss Makepeace's book and the similarities with Digby's.

The professor's ears reddened and his cheeks blew out; it looked as if his whole face could explode. Then he said, "I won't have it. The scandal would finish the society. Digby did it enough harm whilst he was alive, he's certainly not going to deal it a mortal blow from beyond the grave."

There was a stunned silence.

"But what about Miss Makepeace?" asked Darina.

"What about her?" He spoke as though she was not in the room, his glance going everywhere but to her. "How dare she impute the chairman with plagiarism."

"Nicholas"—Rita leant forward in her chair—"have you not considered that her claim could very well be true? My first thought when I read the book last week was where, in the name of the devil, did he find time for all the research? I mean, do you see Digby sitting down to note and analyse every name and its exact use for all the various kinds of mediaeval tarts; darioles, flauns, tarts, coffyns, they're all there."

"Coffyns?" Charles shivered delicately. He was still leaning against the bar but his whole body was taut as a violin string, quivering with the excitement in the room.

"It was only a name used for a container," explained Rita impatiently, "it had no macabre overtones then."

"Digby's in his final container now." Charles gave a gasping sort of giggle.

"A deepe coffyn," murmured Miss Makepeace, then, as they looked at her, added, "that's what recipes used to say, 'make a deepe coffyn.' "

Nicholas ignored her. "I have no doubt that, considering his background and scholarship, Digby was fully capable of getting that book together whatever else he was doing."

"Oh, come on now," protested Rita, "you know as well, if not better, than any of us that Digby's 'scholarship' "—delicate irony suffused the word—"was a thin veneer. The man never evaluated, he absorbed facts and atmosphere as though he were a thirsty sponge, then, with the unerring instincts of a fifties shopgirl, picked the flashy item, went for the good story." She looked challengingly at Nicholas.

He rose from his chair and addressed Miss Makepeace. "You seem to have won over Miss Lisle and Ms. Moore but I have to tell you that I will back Digby Cary's authorship of the book against anyone. As far as I am concerned, your manuscript was lost in the post. It was most careless of you not to have kept a copy and I must ask you not to repeat these baseless accusations without a very real appreciation of the possible legal consequences. No doubt when you are sober, you will see more sense." A jagged purple vein had risen on Nicholas's broad forehead and was throbbing. He directed a burning look at the figure sitting bolt upright in her chair, stubby brown hands clutching at each arm, then turned and left the room.

But as he approached the door, Gray called after him, "Professor, don't do anything hasty, it would be unfortunate were there to be any repetition of the Jameson episode."

Nicholas swung round, his face contorted; he hesitated, struggled to find speech, then gave up and flung himself out of the room.

Linda leapt up and followed him.

Miss Makepeace sank back in her chair, her face chalk white.

"Are you all right?" Darina knelt by her and took one of the weathered hands; it was icy.

"Have a little of this!" Charles thrust another glass of brandy at her.

Miss Makepeace let out a deep breath, looked at the brandy, then jerked out a hand and thrust it away. Liquid splashed over Charles's good hand.

"I've had enough," she announced, "more than enough." The voice was slightly unsteady. "But I know where I stand. I will not give up my fight for my rights. If the professor thinks he can browbeat me, he is mistaken." A small convulsion ran through her and she closed her eyes for a moment. When she opened them, she turned to Darina. "Would it be possible to have a hot milk?" Her voice was a whisper.

Darina nodded. "Of course, Miss Makepeace. Why don't you go up and take one of your sleeping pills and I'll bring it to you in a minute."

The older woman put a hand to her head. "I think I will, my head seems to have two bulls fighting inside it." She rose and took a step towards the door, almost tripping over a small stool.

Charles put out his hand to catch and help her. She knocked it away as she had the glass of brandy. "Don't touch me, you unnatural apology for a man, I need no help." With great dignity, she put her bag under her arm and walked steadily from the room.

"I'd hardly think she needs a sleeping pill. Miss Country Bumpkin should really lay off the booze." Charles's voice was light and vicious, his face white and expressionless. He looked at the glass he'd put down on the table by her chair, picked it up and with a swift movement swallowed what was left. He put it down again and walked out of the bar.

"Well!" said Rita, her green eyes sparkling. "I think I'll just see she gets safely upstairs."

Darina was left studying Gray, the only remaining occupant of the bar. "What did you mean about 'the Jameson episode'?"

He looked slightly uncomfortable. "It may have been a little unfair of me. There was never any proof, but Nicholas seemed so vindictive and Miss Makepeace so defenceless." He doodled on his notebook. Darina waited.

He made up his mind. "It was whilst I was working for my Ph.D. There was some great argument over methodology in the archaeo- logical department; Nicholas was on one side, a new man with a brilliant and growing reputation on the other. Do you know anything about academic arguments and rivalries? Well, they make political in- fighting appear a clean, gentlemanly sport. The whole university seemed to be involved and informed opinion considered that Jame- son had the edge on Nicholas and was about to cast a shadow on the professor's so far spotless and distinguished career. Then, suddenly, Jameson disappeared and Nicholas was left in sole possession of the field. Gradually it seeped out, in the way these things have, that he'd been asked to leave after allegations had been sent anonymously to the college authorities of sexual misconduct with a child."

"And you think it was Nicholas who accused him?"

Gray nodded.

"Was it true?"

"As far as it was possible to find out, probably not. Jameson started proceedings for unlawful dismissal, rumours flew around but I don't think the police ever got to the bottom of the case. It was finally dropped and some months later Jameson was discovered dead from an overdose. There was no note and accidental death was recorded but he'd been unable to find another job and there was a lot of feeling in college. Nicholas acted as though Jameson had deliberately committed suicide to embarrass him. For a time his position was uncertain but there was no proof of anything and eventually matters calmed down as other academic scandals blew up." Gray's voice was level and unemotional but his pencil dug deeply into the paper as it scored lines in a complicated pattern in his notebook. Then the point broke.

He got up and went to the bar. "Can I offer you a drink?"

Darina shook her head. "Thanks, but I must go and organise Miss Makepeace some hot milk. I'll try and find some honey to put in it, I think she could do with a little soothing and cherishing."

He poured himself a large brandy. "She certainly saw off that poisonous worm Childe."

"I thought he would strike her. How on earth are you managing to share a room with him?"

"With difficulty. Now I come to think of it, there's no need any longer, the annexe is full of empty beds. I think I'll move over and take Bracken with me." He tossed back the drink and they left the bar together.

As they entered the main hall, Gray paused. "I think I'll just have a word with the police," he said, knocking on the door of the incident room. Darina looked at him in surprise, then, as the door opened, hurried out of the hall.

SEVENTEEN

Back in the kitchen, Darina put a small saucepan of milk onto the Aga then had a look round for honey. At the back of one of the cupboards she found a jar from Germany. *Tannenhonig* it said under a picture of a beehive. *Honig* must be honey, but what was *Tannen?* Darina ladled a couple of tablespoons into a mug and added the almost boiling milk, stirring to melt the clear, dark stickiness. She licked the spoon. Whatever sort of honey it was, it had a faintly resinous flavour. It was difficult to say whether it was pleasant or not. Darina added a couple of biscuits to the tray.

As she went through the hall, the door to the incident room opened and Sergeant Pigram emerged.

"Miss Lisle," he said pleasantly, "could you spare us a moment, please?"

Darina explained her errand and asked if the question, whatever it was, couldn't wait until after she had delivered her milk. He took the little tray out of her hands, placed it on the hall table, and gently shepherded her into the room. "You can deliver that afterwards," he said.

Both writing tables were covered with neat piles of papers. There were reports, Digby's files and various notes. Both the inspector and the sergeant looked tired.

"Mr. Wyndham has given us details of an incident he thought would interest us," said Grant, waving her to a chair, his voice as clipped and precise as ever. His appearance was still immaculate but William Pigram had loosened his tie and opened the top button of his shirt, and his curly head looked dishevelled.

Darina sat down, her heart sinking. What had Gray been telling them?

"I gather you know more about this matter of Miss Makepeace and the deceased's book than anyone else, perhaps you will give us the full details."

Darina stared at him in surprise. Why had Gray thought it necessary to inform them? Did he really think Miss Makepeace could be the murderer? Or was he trying to alert them to Nicholas and how jealous he could be of his position?

Gathering her wandering wits, Darina gave a concise account of the conversation she'd overheard the previous night and her discussion with Miss Makepeace that evening. When she'd finished the inspector sat and looked at her for a minute. Then he said, "You realise you are guilty of withholding what could be material evidence in a murder case?"

Somewhat lamely Darina explained she hadn't thought it relevant.

Grant sighed wearily. "Perhaps you will let me be the judge of what could be relevant."

"Anyway," went on Darina with a touch of defiance, "if I had told you, wouldn't you have thought I was trying to deflect suspicion from myself?" And was that what Gray had been doing?

The inspector regarded her with his cold eyes. "It is not up to you to prejudge our reactions to evidence," he said. He seemed about to say something else, then thought better of it. "All right, you can go," he finished crisply.

Darina could feel his eyes following her to the door. As she opened it, he called her back. "One more thing, we have received further information about the deceased's estate."

"I know about the trust fund," she said shortly.

"Do you indeed? Do you also know that the Chelsea house does not form part of it? That will come to you. And are you aware it is probably worth some three-quarters of a million pounds?" He watched her with calculating eyes.

Darina felt very tired. The events of the day had been unsettling to say the least and she had had a very early start. The implications of being left Digby's house were beyond her.

"If that's all . . ." she said and opened the door. Neither policeman stopped her.

Darina picked up the mug of milk. It had lost most of its heat. Sighing, she returned to the kitchen, poured the milk back into the saucepan, reheated it, refilled the mug and took it upstairs.

Looking tired but unsleepy, Miss Makepeace was in bed, a volumi-
nous Viyella nightie covering her compact body. Her glasses had
been removed and without them her eyes were owl-naked and vulnerable.

She took the mug. "How kind, m'dear. Mary would often bring me
hot milk, it always settled me." She took a pill from a bottle on the
bedside table, put it in her mouth and swallowed it without water.
"It is so hard to realise she's gone. I never took pills before she died.
Don't really hold with such things. But I wasn't getting any sleep at
all and the doctor told me it wasn't sensible." She sipped the milk.
"That's an odd flavour, what is it?"

Darina explained about the German honey.

"Oh, that'll be made from firs."

Of course, thought Darina, *Tannenbaum,* the fir tree.

"We saw it on sale during our Black Forest holiday," went on Miss
Makepeace, sitting back on her pillow and looking more relaxed. "It
was the first and only holiday Mary and I took together. We enjoyed
ourselves so much. If we managed to scrape up the money, we were
going to go abroad again this year. The ways of the Lord are sometimes hard to understand." She smoothed the sheet with one of her
brown hands.

"Isn't it something to have had at least one holiday together to
remember?" Darina asked tentatively.

The brown eyes studied her. "I hadn't thought of it like that. Now
there's something for me to consider as I try to get to sleep, it might
even take my mind off that wretched book." Her eyes sharpened,
peering at Darina. "If you see the professor again tonight, you can
tell him I am going to fight for my rights. He needn't think he can
browbeat me."

"Bravo," applauded Darina.

Miss Makepeace held out the mug to her. "Thank you, m'dear,
I've finished it, but I'm glad I didn't buy any of that honey. But it was
most kind of you to bring me the drink," she added hastily.

"Can I get you anything else?"

"No, thank you, I should settle nicely now."

As Darina came down the stairs to the first-floor landing, Linda
rushed up, her face flushed and eyes red. "Have you seen Nicholas?"
she demanded. "Oh God," she burst out as Darina shook her head,

"I can't find him anywhere. He went outside after he left the bar, wouldn't wait for me and I lost him in the dark. It's all the fault of that wretched woman. Just as we were getting on so well." Her voice was a moan and tears started to well up in her already swollen eyes. Before Darina could say anything, she turned away and dashed along the corridor, into her room, slamming the door behind her.

Darina sighed and continued downstairs.

In the kitchen she placed the mug in the dishwasher, cleaned the saucepan and checked the arrangements for the morning. As she was wondering how many policemen she should cater for, there was a tap on the door and in came the tall sergeant carrying a tray of dirty plates.

"We've finished for today," he said, putting the tray on the table, then picking up the crockery and bringing it to the sink, "and I thought it might help if I brought these down."

"How kind, no, don't put them there, they'll go in the dishwasher." Darina opened the door of the machine, took them from his hands and started stacking them in.

"Seeing the staff you had helping, I thought you probably didn't have one of these," he said, bringing over the glasses.

"The trouble is, it takes too long to do its cycle, it's not a proper commercial catering machine." Darina closed the door. "Can I get you anything? Coffee? Tea?"

"Or hot milk?" he grinned at her. "Thank you, coffee would be more than welcome." He took a seat at the table and watched her pull up the cover of the Aga hot-plate and put the kettle on. He leant back in the chair with his hands linked behind his head, as at ease as though he was in his own kitchen.

Darina asked if the inspector would also like some coffee as she got the beans out and put them in the grinder. For a brief moment the morning came back to her with Nicholas complaining of the noise.

Then the sergeant spoke and the memory faded. "No, he's gone over to the annexe, leaving me to lock up here. I'm in the room Digby Cary had, forensics finished with it this afternoon. That's so that if there's any trouble in the night, I'm the one who'll have his sleep disturbed."

How friendly he looked now he'd shed the official, intimidating air

he had worn earlier that evening in the incident room with the
inspector. "Trouble?" She whirred the beans then poured the ground
coffee into a *cafetière*.

"Oh, attacks by dogs, verbal maulings by professors, that sort of
thing."

She found herself laughing. The kettle boiled; she took it off,
waited a moment, then poured the hot water onto the grounds,
added the plunger on top and brought the pot over to the table with
a couple of mugs. She left the *cafetière* for a moment or two then
carefully pushed down the plunger and poured out the coffee. The
sergeant refused milk or sugar or a biscuit.

"Nanny told me never to eat between meals."

Darina eyed his lean length. "You hardly have to worry about
weight, surely?"

"They say every pound you put on before thirty-five becomes five
at fifty," he said sententiously. As Darina dragged up another smile,
he looked at her closely. "You must be dead on your feet, it's been a
hell of a day for you." There was real sympathy in his voice.

"Oh, finding a dead body, producing lunch for sixty or so and
becoming chief suspect in a murder investigation is all in the day's
work for me," she said brightly.

"We have to consider the evidence," he said gently. "By the way,
there *was* an identifiable print of yours on that knife, on the blade
just above the haft. The handle was wiped clean, of course."

"I do understand about evidence but what about people, don't you
have to consider character as well?"

He looked down into his mug. "There's the real nub of the matter.
Crimes *are* committed by people, people with hang-ups, desires,
fears. People conditioned by their upbringing, by circumstances. But
people are sometimes forced out of their normal behaviour by a
threat or an event. Under stress, they can give way to totally foreign
reactions. So whilst we try to understand the people involved, we
have to start with the evidence. And at the end of the day, it's facts
that are dealt with in court. Where character is very important is
with consideration of motive. What can move one person to murder
can be of minor interest to another."

Darina sat and thought and he sat and watched her.

"So you try and tie in evidence with what the suspects reveal to you of themselves," she said.

"Something like that. We build up a picture of the deceased, his character, his circumstances. Often money is at the bottom of a crime, so we look at who would benefit from the deceased's death and if they were in need of cash. Jealousy is an equally strong motive, revenge another . . ." He paused.

"Go on," pressed Darina.

"At the same time," he continued, holding the mug in both his hands as though they were cold, "we look at all the evidence and the statements in minute detail, trying to see beyond the obvious. Sometimes what a witness says betrays things he doesn't know he's telling you."

"Like what?"

He thought for a moment, then grinned at her. "You told us this evening you knew about Lady Sarah's trust fund. We could deduce from that you must have had a conversation with Mr. Wyndham, since he was the only one who could have told you."

"But you knew that," objected Darina. "You saw us coming up from the lake together."

"But suppose I hadn't," he said, "and suppose you had told us you'd spent the entire afternoon peeling potatoes alone in the kitchen?"

"I don't think I'd have told you I knew about the trust fund if that had been the case," said Darina doubtfully.

"No, you might have been clear-headed enough to see its implications. Not everyone is, or their mind is too taken up with other considerations to realise exactly what they are letting out of the bag." He returned his gaze to his coffee mug and added gently, "It also told us other things about you and Mr. Wyndham."

"Such as what?" Darina was not sure she wanted to hear this.

"That you had made friends in a very short time, that he was someone you could talk to and that you might feel a certain loyalty to him when it came to describing actions of his or his involvement with other members of the society."

Darina sat and let the implications of what this quiet policeman had said sink in. She forgot her tiredness. She became aware that the currents and tensions running through the group of suspects could be seen in a new light. She began to look at their statements and actions in a way the police might, seeing that they could illuminate not only character and motive but also deceive in a way that could be illuminating in itself. She looked back over the day and became aware of light and shade playing over the events, throwing certain actions and statements into relief, allowing others to sink into the background. Large chunks of the landscape of events started to drift and move like prehistoric landmasses, disturbing accepted patterns and making new.

"It matters to me that my cousin's murderer should be caught," she said.

He nodded, accepting the logic behind her seeming non-sequitur. "I know, it matters to us, too."

She looked straight at him. "Do you believe I could have done it?"

He returned the look steadily. "No, I don't."

"And the inspector?"

He smiled wryly and gave a graceful little wave of his hand that apologised for what was coming next. "Let's say it's a possibility he has to keep in mind. He can't afford the luxury of believing in people."

"So what does he believe in?"

"Facts. It works the other way, too, you know. It means he doesn't get convinced someone *is* a murderer without the evidence to back it up."

"So he's not going to arrest me yet?"

The sergeant shook his head. "Not without considerably more evidence than we have at the moment."

She sat and studied him, not having taken in much beyond his height and dark, curly hair before this. She saw a thin, intelligent face with a wide mouth, pulled down at one corner in a self-deprecating way; the nose was aquiline and the grey eyes the colour of herrings, their silvery sparkle flecked with dark. They held a quizzical look as he sat silent before her scrutiny, his hands with their long, broad-ended fingers lying either side of the now empty mug.

"Why did you become a policeman?" Darina asked the question abruptly, trying to identify why she didn't think he looked like one.

"A misplaced desire to meddle in things that don't concern me," he said lightly.

"Seriously?"

He continued to return her gaze, then something altered in his face. "You really want to know, don't you?"

She nodded.

"I went into the Foreign Office when I came down from Oxford; I was all set to become our man in Paris, Moscow or Peking. But after a couple of years pushing pens in minor legations, I thought I wanted to be where the action was a good deal sharper. So I went into the City and for a bit I enjoyed the pressure, the excitement, the money. Then I began to wonder exactly what I was doing and what was going to happen when I reached forty, burnt out and either a millionaire or bankrupt. When I started thinking, I realised what I cared about was people, that it was concern for our relationships with people that had taken me into the Foreign Office, only vanity and greed had got in the way. My father knows the Chief Constable of our county and I had a long talk with him about life in the police force and finally joined up."

Now Darina could understand why he didn't add up to her idea of a policeman. "Has it lived up to your expectations?"

He grinned again, his momentary seriousness gone. "Some of the time. Especially since I've become detective sergeant to Inspector Grant. He's a mean man in many ways, and will call me Bill, and believes in giving his staff a hard time but he's sharp as the claw of a tiger, nothing escapes him. I've learned more in the three months I've worked with him than all the rest of my time in the force."

Darina offered more coffee and, as he held out his mug for a refill, he said, "We could do with you on our team, you have a knack for getting people to talk. It's a great asset in our job."

Which reminded Darina of something. "Is it possible to go into the housekeeper's room yet?"

"Something you want there?"

"Not really, I was just wondering, that's all." Darina felt she could hardly tell a detective sergeant of police she wanted to check the position of a murder victim.

He eyed her. "You're up to something, I can tell. As far as I know, they will finish in there tomorrow morning."

Which led to the question of how many police would require lunch the next day.

"You don't have to feed us," he said gently. "Not that we aren't grateful, we shall have withdrawal symptoms when we leave here."

"Shall we be able to leave tomorrow?"

"Ah, that's not for me to say but I think it's more than likely."

"You mean you'll know who the murderer is by then?"

He shook his head regretfully. "I doubt it. We have the murder weapon, there's no mystery about the how, only the who and the why. So many of you had the opportunity, more and more of you appear to have a motive and there's precious little evidence to link anyone with the killing." He paused for a moment, then added, "I shouldn't really be talking to you like this; Grant would have forty thousand fits if he could hear me."

"I'm the soul of discretion," Darina assured him gravely.

"I believe you are." He sat looking at her for a little longer, then said, "I'm going to ask you to be a little less discreet with me."

"In what way?"

"As I said, you have a knack for getting people to talk. I am quite sure you have found out all sorts of things about the other people here that could help us enormously."

Darina stared at him.

"I know," he went on, "you think that's like sneaking, telling tales out of school and all that. That's why you didn't tell us about Miss Makepeace's confrontation with Digby Cary. But forget that, think of it instead as helping to catch your cousin's murderer. As not allowing the criminal to get away with his crime. You can't be expected to know what is important and what irrelevant, we are trained to assess just that."

He made her realise she had been seeing the police as on one side and she and the symposiasts on another. That she had been treating them as adversaries, to be told no more than was absolutely essential. Was it because they had treated her as a prime suspect? For surely she and they were both on the same side. They both wanted to discover who had killed Digby.

"Put that way," Darina said slowly, "you make it impossible to refuse." But, she thought to herself, I no longer like you quite so much.

Slowly she began to tell him details of the various conversations she had been involved with during that long, long day.

She told him about Gray's need for money, his love for Digby's wife. She told him of Rita's long affair with Digby, and Linda's. She told him how worried Miss Makepeace was about something to do with the dog incident; how resentful Nicholas had seemed at Digby's success and his extraordinarily strong reaction to the charge of plagiarism against Digby by Miss Makepeace. And about the clash of methodologies that had ended in the death of another professor.

"And that's about it," she finished. "Charles you probably know more of than I do. All I've gathered about him is that his restaurant is probably not too successful and that if Digby had left *him* his money, he would be considered a hot suspect. He doesn't seem to know a great deal about cooking, either, despite that television series," she added.

What television series, William Pigram wanted to know, so Darina told him about that as well. By the end, she felt drained. And she didn't like herself. Despite her desire to have the murderer caught, she felt, just as the sergeant had suggested, a sneak—worse, a traitor. She had told the police details that would probably not have been revealed to her had she been in their uniform. It made her a spy.

"I'm sorry." The sergeant reached across and laid his hand on hers. Darina snatched it away, feeling childish but unable to stop herself. "I know it won't help but I have to tell you that you have only done your duty, both as a citizen and by your cousin."

Darina said nothing, but got up, stacked their mugs in the dishwasher, switched it on and checked the Aga was turned down.

William Pigram opened the kitchen door that gave onto the back corridor. "Did you say the professor was outside? I'll see if I can track him down, I'd like a breath of fresh air before turning in."

"Good-night, Sergeant," said Darina stiffly.

"Call me William." He lifted his hand in a salute then disappeared out of the back door.

EIGHTEEN

Darina walked upstairs. Though her body was so tired she had difficulty remembering how to pull one leg up after the other, her mind was still functioning in overdrive. Her recital to the sergeant, however reluctantly wrung from her, had made certain patterns emerge with greater clarity. But somewhere she was sure she was missing a detail that was highly significant. Was it a snatch of conversation? If so, what had it been and who had said it?

She reached her room and, after a bit of searching, found a piece of paper and a pencil. What was needed was a timetable of events. That was what all the detective novels she had read contained.

She'd told the police she gave Nicholas the message from Digby just after ten minutes past eleven. She could pinpoint that because the tart had just been put in the oven and she had checked the time. Digby must have been alive then; she'd been with him in the housekeeper's room only ten minutes or so before.

What had happened then? She had returned to the kitchen and started preparations for the next day. She hadn't seen anyone come down but apparently Rita, at least, had gone into the housekeeper's room via the corridor. When?

The party in the bar must have broken up immediately after she had gone back to the kitchen. Rita had said she'd gone upstairs to collect her notes before going to find Digby. So, write 11:15 to 11:20 Rita Moore arrives in housekeeper's room. Her confrontation with Digby had lasted, according to her, about twelve minutes. So add: 11:30–11:35 Rita Moore returns to hall, goes up staircase to bed.

Darina thought for a moment, then inserted: 11:15 Gray Wyndham collects dog from boiler room, takes him out through front door. He obviously hadn't seen Rita, so she could cross out 11:15 for her arrival at the housekeeper's room, leaving it at 11:20.

What about Charles? He had apparently come down at some stage and heard Rita and Digby quarrelling. So put: 11:25–11:30 Charles Childe in corridor outside housekeeper's room. Darina's pencil paused. Had he lingered outside the door or returned immediately? Rita hadn't seen him. Darina placed a question mark beside his timing, then, on a new line, put: 11:45 DL goes to bed.

She'd gone out of the kitchen door nearest the stairs without seeing anyone but that didn't mean there hadn't been someone out of sight, round the bend in the corridor. Or with Digby.

For the first time, Darina regretted she had not gone to say goodnight to Digby. If she had, would he be alive now? Or had the murderer arrived after she had gone to bed?

12:05–12:10, Darina wrote, Charles Childe comes down staircase and is attacked by Bracken.

12:10–12:15 Gray Wyndham returns Bracken to boiler room, does not close door properly.

When had he arrived in Rita's bathroom? Darina chewed the end of the pencil for a bit then wrote down: 12:20–12:25 Gray arrives Rita's room.

12:45 Gray Wyndham goes downstairs to collect car.

12:50 Charles taken downstairs and put in Gray's car.

Darina thought some more. She hadn't made entries for Nicholas going up to bed or Miss Makepeace and Linda. And what about Miss Makepeace's appearance on the landing? Was that after Darina had gone downstairs, or had she looked over during the few moments Darina had lain in bed wondering about the commotion? She slotted in a general dispersal to bedrooms 11:10–11:15 and then added: 12:08 or 12:12 Miss Makepeace looks over banisters; 12:10 DL goes downstairs.

Darina sat and studied her timetable. The exact timings might be a little awry but the sequence must be reasonably accurate. What did it tell her?

She put a couple of big asterisks and three question marks in the gap between 11:45 and just after midnight. What had happened during that time? Had the murderer come down after Rita had gone back to bed, killed Digby and returned upstairs before Charles had come down just after midnight? Or had the murder taken place after that time?

But then there would have been the question of the dog. When had he got loose? Had he taken a little time to realise he could release himself from his prison? Had it been the sound of someone coming down that had incited him to work his way out? But if so, surely he would have made a great commotion?

It was time for a new approach.

Darina took another sheet of paper and wrote down all the suspects' names, then wrote beside each the opportunity they had had to commit the murder plus their motive.

The list looked like this:

SUSPECT	OPPORTUNITY	MOTIVE
Gray Wyndham	On collecting dog at 11:15? Very little time. On returning dog at 12:10?	Desire to revenge Sarah and/or need of trust fund
Rita Moore	During her confrontation with Digby	Revenge, frustrated desire
Nicholas Turvey	After Rita had left. Or after Charles & Gray had left if Bracken still inside boiler room	Jealousy
Linda Stainmore	Same as Nicholas	Jealousy, revenge, frustrated desire
Charles Childe	After Rita had left. Q. If so, what was he doing coming downstairs again when Gray & Bracken returned from their walk? Had he forgotten something incriminating. If so, the police hadn't found it yet	Desire to suppress Digby's column, hatred of Digby. Q. Did he hate Digby?
Miss Makepeace	After Rita had left. Or after Gray & Charles had left if Bracken, etc.	Revenge

Darina compared her two lists. What a pity there wasn't any way of knowing how long Bracken had taken to find his way out of the boiler room. Perhaps Gray could give her some idea how quickly he picked up new tricks. Unless he was the murderer.

The most unlikely suspect was undoubtedly the last. So, if this was a detective story, Miss Makepeace would probably turn out to be the murderer. But the timings seemed tricky. She would have had to come down from the second floor and return up there again after doing the deed. One the other hand, she had been out of her room when Charles Childe went downstairs. Had she just returned from a trip to the housekeeper's room?

Darina banished the ridiculous thought and rubbed her eyes. There was little point in flogging her brains any further that night. Sleep would be much more profitable. She reached for her toilet bag and headed for the bathroom.

But as she at last got into bed, her thoughts returned again to Miss Makepeace. What an amazing woman she was. Such dedication, to take her degree then amass her research so painstakingly over so many years. How could she have had her trust in Digby so cruelly abused?

But, then, Darina's trust had also been abused. She lay in bed, finally unable to block out any longer the memory of the night her faith in her cousin had been shattered beyond repair.

It had been six months before Sarah's cancer was diagnosed. Digby had returned unexpectedly early from a trip abroad and Sarah was still at Dorrington. He'd rung Darina and suggested they go out for a meal together if she was free. It had been a pleasant evening with Digby at his most charming and she'd accepted his suggestion of a drink back at the house, thinking this was the ideal opportunity to persuade him to make more of an effort to spend time with Sarah and keep his name out of the gossip columns. Instead, she found herself fending off a seduction attempt that outclassed anything Mills and Boon could dream up.

He'd settled her on the comfortable sofa in the drawing room, so charmingly furnished with carefully polished antiques; opened the linen press where they kept the drinks and filled two brandy balloons with generous measures from an opaque black bottle.

"Try this, let me know what you think," he'd said, sitting beside her.

She'd held the glass, swirling the liquid gently round the sides, letting the warmth of her hand release the spirit's bouquet, feeling relaxed and contented in the familiar room. She was happy to be so in tune with Digby, a circumstance that had become rarer and rarer as she had watched the pain he caused Sarah. And seen the deterioration in his character as he grew in power in the food world.

But that night nothing disturbed the peace of the evening as she buried her nose in the depths of the glass, letting the fumes of the powerful spirit intoxicate her. Then she raised her head, surprised. "That's not brandy, surely?"

Digby looked pleased. "What do you think it is?"

She sniffed it again, then took a mouthful, letting it roll around her tongue, allowing her taste buds to assess its flavour to the full. Finally she asked hesitantly, "Rum?"

"Right! It's a twelve-year-old vintage rum. Just about to be launched on the market. Good, isn't it?"

Darina sipped it with pleasure, then found the glass removed from her hand and Digby placing it beside his own on a table behind the sofa. Even then she had no inkling of what was to come, not until he ran his hand gently under the long fair hair and caressed the nape of her neck.

"Darina, darling, I've waited so long for this, you're so beautiful," and he'd pulled her towards him with an easy power, bringing his mouth down on hers, gently at first, then, as realisation dawned and she attempted to pull away, with increasing passion.

Even now, nearly two years later, Darina couldn't bring herself to remember the full details of what followed. It had involved the use of all her strength, torn clothing, bloody scratches down one side of Digby's face (and how was he going to explain those to Sarah, she'd thought agonisedly even as her fingers deliberately raked his cheek), before he realised he wasn't going to be able to have his way.

"You're a fool," he said at last as she stood against the fireplace, holding her blouse together with shaking fingers, the other hand grasping a poker she'd snatched up and now brandished at him with every intention of using if he tried again. "You know you feel as I do, we belong together."

"And what about Sarah?" Darina dragged the words out, exhaustion slurring their edges but their meaning unmistakable.

Digby attempted to control his rapid breathing and restore his clothing to some degree of respectability. "Sarah has nothing to do with us. She understands that there are things I need she can't provide."

"Well, isn't that nice for you!" Scorn sharpened Darina's ability to speak despite the trembling that had invaded every part of her body. "You allow her to provide every comfort"—her glance took in the elegance of the room—"then calmly take your pleasures elsewhere. I can't understand why she stays with you. She's worth ten of you— no, a hundred."

Unaccountably, Digby got angry. "I won't hear you speak of Sarah in that way!"

"You disgust me, Digby. Whatever I may once have felt for you is quite dead. Don't ever try to prove otherwise."

With that she'd left, forgetting her bag, just snatching up her coat from the hall chair. She'd had to walk home. If it had been three times the distance, she could not have brought herself to go back and retrieve her money for a taxi.

Digby had sent the bag back next morning. She never knew how he explained the scratches. For some time Darina had made excuses when asked to visit until Sarah had asked point-blank why she was avoiding them. She'd accepted the next invitation and gradually a semblance of normality had returned to her relationship with Digby.

When he'd suggested she assist with the cooking at the first Annual Symposium of the Society of Historical Gastronomes, she had accepted with misgivings. But he had behaved perfectly. Not until after Sarah's death had he attempted to approach her again, when he'd found an implacable resistance.

Now he was dead too. Murdered with a boning knife.

Now Darina could only feel a desperate need to discover his killer. It was as though the violent act had cauterised the suppurating wound of his betrayal.

Darina lay very still in her bed and finally recognised that part of the revulsion and disgust she had felt that evening two years ago was because she had actually wanted Digby to make love to her. She had had to fight not only her cousin but also her own body.

Then the tears came, for the Digby she had loved, who had remained buried within the carapace of the polished personality; the charismatic young man with a burning ambition and love of food who had found it impossible to resist any of the goodies a generous life had offered him.

The tears wet upon her face, she finally fell into an exhausted sleep.

NINETEEN

The shrill pulsing of Darina's little alarm clock did not go off until 6:45 A.M. The few extra minutes of sleep had had little effect on her tiredness. She lay in bed, gradually letting the outside world filter through to her consciousness, trying to summon up the energy to leave the warm comfort.

Rain was pattering on the window, grey light seeping through the thin curtains. Blocks of darkness on the walls identified the pictures of between-the-wars gardens that decorated the room. The back of an upright chair in front of the dressing table was outlined in silhouette.

Darina sighed. This time yesterday morning she had been about to discover Digby's body, had experienced the last few moments of a smoothly running conference, unaware that the whole weekend was about to be turned upside down and her life with it.

Without notice, from the depths of her subconscious, like a slice of truffle in sparkling clear consommé, up floated the snippet of conversation her exhausted mind had been fishing for the previous night. And she understood the meaning of the phrase, "her blood ran cold." For all heat seemed to drain out of her body and a deadly, clammy chill took over.

Unmoving, she examined the fact, if fact it was. If it meant what she thought it did, she had found the murderer. Or had she? Might it not just mean another undisclosed visit to Digby? But how many more could there be and still leave time for yet another by the murderer? And there was an awful inevitability about the identity.

Other snippets of conversation from the weekend joined the first, rounding out the picture. Conviction filled Darina. She had found the killer.

Slowly she got up, slipped on her dressing gown and went to the bathroom. She turned on the taps and allowed hot water to pour into the bath. Gratefully she lowered herself into its comforting warmth and gradually felt her body lose its chill. She felt more tired than ever but quite calm.

The problem now was where to go from here, how to prove it. She had no concrete evidence, nothing she could take to the police. Her mind shied away from her late-night interview with Sergeant Pigram.

For interview it had been. How could she have thought he was merely being friendly when he entered her kitchen and accepted coffee? And yet, she had to admit he had clarified her thinking about the crime.

As the heat of the water relaxed her body, another thought drifted into her mind. William Pigram would not be able to accept what she had told him at its face value. He would have to look at it sideways, just as she had learned to look again at everything she had heard ever since this symposium had started. He would have to consider that she could have been misleading him, might have misunderstood what she had been told, allowed prejudices to colour her recollections. For some reason, she found the thought comforting.

Reluctantly she left the relaxing warmth of the bath, dried and dressed herself, then went downstairs.

Frumenty had been scheduled for Sunday breakfast but, in the drama of yesterday, Darina had forgotten all about soaking the cracked wheat, so the porridge-like confection would have to be abandoned. That left herb omelette, pancakes and devilled kidneys to prepare.

As she turned up the Aga, Darina wondered whether people wouldn't actually prefer boiled eggs and soldiers, then banished the thought. They had come here to eat period food and eat it they would, no matter how many murders were committed. She started her preparations.

Nobody seemed to have lost their appetite. The hot dishes were plundered heartily. Nicholas and Linda had entered the refectory together and seemed in harmony with each other again. They were sitting at one end of the table Darina had laid, chatting happily about plans for the programme on Digby.

Rita had a plate piled high with food which she was eating with evident enjoyment. Charles Childe had been more restrained and had seated himself next to the sergeant. As she retrieved empty dishes, Darina could hear him relating interminable details about his restaurant. William Pigram was listening with every appearance of deep interest.

She took her tray towards the kitchen. As she reached the foot of the stairs, there was the sound of excited barking. Darina went round the corner of the corridor and saw Gray with Bracken, followed by the inspector. The dog greeted her with more eager barking and pulled against the lead, almost dragging it out of his master's hand in his enthusiasm to get to her.

Darina placed her tray on top of one of the cupboards that lined the corridor and bent to caress him.

"You've made a friend for life here," said Gray. He looked as though he hadn't slept well, his eyes tired, their pouches sagging even more than usual. He opened the boiler room door and dragged in the reluctant dog.

The inspector was as neat and dapper as if he had slept a full eight hours in a first-class hotel. He nodded a good morning and continued straight on to the refectory.

Darina picked up her tray. The back door opened again and Linda's camera team came in, pleading for breakfast.

"There are extra places laid in the refectory and I'm just about to take some fresh food up," said Darina.

When she entered the refectory with more pancakes, omelette and kidneys, there was a pleasant buzz. The tensions of the previous night seemed to have evaporated. No one, though, seemed to be talking to the inspector. He was efficiently disposing of devilled kidneys and herb omelette, making no attempt to strike up a conversation with Rita, who was sitting on his left. The place on his right was unoccupied.

Darina looked round the table. Miss Makepeace was missing. Usually she was amongst the first down for breakfast—was she still under the influence of her sleeping pills? Well, there was no reason why she shouldn't sleep late, she probably needed the extra hour or so.

No one showed any desire to rush breakfast. The first to move was the inspector, glancing at his sergeant as he rose. Responding to his cue, William got up too and looked at Linda.

"Miss Stainmore, could you spare us a little time in, say, ten minutes?"

Linda smiled nervously. Her face was the colour of the chunky white beads filling the neckline of a vivid red dress. Nicholas gave her hand an absent-minded pat. "It'll be perfectly straightforward," he said. Linda did not look reassured.

Darina checked the teapot and took it back with her to the kitchen for a refill. As the kettle came to the boil, she started laying a tray. She would take breakfast up to Miss Makepeace.

Some fifteen minutes later she knocked on the bedroom door. There was no answer. She knocked again, louder, and called, "Miss Makepeace, it's Darina Lisle, I've brought you some breakfast." Finally she turned the handle and gently pushed the door open.

The room was dark with the curtains tightly drawn. She switched on the light. Miss Makepeace was still asleep; Darina could hear heavy breathing. She put the tray on the dressing table, austerely furnished with hairbrush and comb and a bottle of toning lotion, then drew the curtains. The rain had stopped. Wind was blowing away the clouds and the sun had begun to shine. It had the makings of a nice day.

Miss Makepeace had still not stirred. Darina went and gently shook her shoulder, then snatched back her hand as the sleeping woman rolled unresistingly onto her back with her mouth open, her eyes shut and oddly sunken, her breath now noisily stertorous. The upper lip quivered as the breath snorted out through her mouth with unnatural force.

Darina took hold of Miss Makepeace by the shoulder and shook her, first gently and then more roughly. The head lolled sideways on the pillow like that of a dead rabbit discarded by a marauding dog. She called her name several times, almost shouting into an ear that seemed to hear nothing. She rubbed the back of her finger against the weatherbeaten cheek, as her father used to do when he wanted to wake her. Miss Makepeace did not wake. If anything, she seemed to slip further into sleep. Darina felt a panic start to build in the pit of her stomach. She made up her mind, moved quickly out of the room and ran down the stairs, into the incident room, not pausing to knock on the door. Inside, Grant looked up with annoyance, William Pigram with concern and Linda with interest.

"It's Miss Makepeace," Darina said, "we need to call a doctor, immediately!" The room slipped its focus and she grabbed the back of a chair.

She was aware of the inspector pushing past her out of the room, calling back over his shoulder, "Organise a doctor, Bill, and an ambulance, don't leave the room." She sank into the chair and heard the sergeant start telephoning.

"What has happened to Miss Makepeace?" Linda was in total control, the news producer on the track of a story.

"I'm not sure." Darina pulled herself together. "She seems to have lost consciousness, I can't wake her."

"Overdose of sleeping tablets?" Linda enquired clinically, then became more excited. "Could she have murdered Digby and decided to take her own life?"

"I don't think we should speculate," William Pigram said quietly, replacing the receiver.

Linda fished a small book out of her bag with a pencil and started to make some notes.

The sergeant picked up the telephone again. As he instructed the hospital where to send the ambulance, his eyes switched to Darina. Her breathing had returned to normal and the room had stopped turning.

As the telephone was replaced for the second time, the inspector returned to the room. "Organised that doctor, Bill?"

"Should be here in a few minutes, sir," the sergeant said.

The front door bell sounded.

"That's too soon for the doc, must be the forensic boys. Bill, let them in and ask Watson and Stanton to come in here."

A large, untidy man Darina remembered seeing in the housekeeper's room the day before came in with the detective sergeant followed by a thinner man with greying hair.

"Watson, I want you to stay here with Miss Stainmore. Under no circumstances is she to talk to any of the others or to make any telephone calls. Stanton, when the doctor arrives, bring him up to the second floor, third door on the right, and no dawdling, it could mean the difference between life and death." There was no drama in his level voice as he gave the instructions. "Miss Lisle, come with us."

Grant led the way out of the room and up the staircase. He

seemed to have made himself very familiar with the layout, Darina thought, hurrying in his wake. Without seeming to move fast, he climbed the stairs exceedingly rapidly.

When they reached Miss Makepeace's room, Darina stood in the doorway and watched him and the sergeant walk across to the bed. Miss Makepeace hadn't moved. Her breathing was, if anything, even noisier than before.

Grant reached for her pulse and lifted one eyelid. He straightened himself. "That ambulance had better hurry," he said.

His gaze moved over the room, finally coming to rest on the bed-side table. It held a small bottle with the top off. He tilted it with a pencil out of his inside pocket. "Two left," he said and studied the label.

He stood quite still for a moment then turned to Darina. "How much did she have to drink last night?"

"Two, no, three glasses of wine, maybe a little more, I'm not sure how much she had with dinner, and a brandy afterwards."

"How was she when you brought the milk up last night?" William Pigram asked.

Grant's head came up. "What's this?"

His sergeant explained about Darina's interrupted errand the previous evening. Grant asked her to describe the incident in detail.

She was in the middle of her account when Stanton brought in the doctor. He hurried to the bed, setting his bag on the floor and, like Grant, lifted one of Miss Makepeace's eyelids.

"Take Miss Lisle back to the incident room, Stanton, then return here," said Grant.

The sound of Miss Makepeace's breathing followed them down the stairs. Darina tried to feel it was a hopeful sign.

Linda had finished making her notes and was sitting, obviously fuming with impatience, before the solid gaze of Watson, who was impassively occupying a chair at the side of the room.

Darina sat in another and did what she could to stall Linda's excited questioning. She refused to offer a possible explanation for Miss Makepeace's condition, refused to speculate on the likelihood of a deliberate overdose of sleeping tablets. But in the uncomfortable silence that followed, she desperately tried to recall the tablet bottle as Miss Makepeace had taken her pill the previous evening. How many had it held? Had it rattled with more than one or two? But it was no use, all she knew was that one had been taken whilst she had been in the room.

An ambulance passed the window and came to rest outside the front door. Linda rose and went to the window; Darina followed and stood behind her.

Two attendants got out with a stretcher and were ushered inside. A few minutes later the stretcher was carefully manipulated into the rear of the ambulance bearing a surprisingly small form covered by a thick red blanket. Darina could just glimpse a white face before the stretcher passed out of her view. The doors were shut and then the vehicle pulled away with a dramatic spray of gravel and the wail of a siren.

Stanton reappeared and took her upstairs again.

Grant and Pigram were beside the now empty bed, the clothes turned back in an untidy pile. The doctor was examining the label of the bottle on the bedside table.

"How is she?" asked Darina.

"Touch and go," said the doctor. "Excuse me, Inspector, I'd better get on to the hospital. Looks like an overdose of sleeping pills but if that bottle contained what it says on the label, she'd have needed an astonishingly large number, they're very mild. There is the alcohol she had last night, of course, that would potentiate their effect. I'll let you know how things go as soon as I can." He snapped his case shut and left the room.

Grant turned to Darina. "Finish your account of last night."

After she'd stumbled through the rest of her story, he turned back to the bottle by the bed. "And those are the pills she took?"

"Pill," said Darina, "I only saw her take one."

He looked at her searchingly. "What sort of mood was she in?"

"Difficult to say, she'd drunk more than I would guess was usual for her. She was missing her sister; she'd died some months ago and I think they were very close. But she was full of determination to gain recognition of her book."

"Hmm, depression could have overtaken her after you left, particularly after all that alcohol, and she could have taken more then. But why leave two pills in the bottle, why not take them all? And there's no glass of water."

"She could have gone to the bathroom?" suggested William Pigram.

"She swallowed the one I saw her take without water," said Darina.

Grant threw another look round the room. "Is there anything different from when you left last night?" he asked.

She looked around. With its dishevelled bedclothes, the room seemed vandalised but she could detect nothing materially different and said so.

"Right"—Grant gave a last glance around—"let's go back downstairs. Miss Lisle, I've finished with you for the moment but don't do any disappearing act."

"I have lunch to cook."

The inspector sighed. "Far too much attention is paid to food by everyone concerned in this case." He directed a pointed look at his sergeant, who appeared oblivious as he led the way downstairs.

In the refectory, the symposiasts were full of the new drama. Darina received the sort of reception Paul Revere must have met with from the American revolutionists, only she had no information as dramatic to impart.

". . . and that's all I know," she said finally.

"Well, it looks as though she won't be making waves in your precious society after all." Charles threw a look of sparkling malice towards Nicholas.

He was gazing vacantly at the table. "What do you mean?"

"Digby's book! If she doesn't make it, she can't insist it's hers!"

"I hope she will make it," Darina said tartly and went off to the kitchen.

Rita followed her. "What are her chances?" she asked as she caught Darina up in the corridor.

"God knows, her pulse was terribly weak but she's a strong person, in every sense."

Darina opened the kitchen door. Rita turned back, then bumped into Nicholas, who had appeared with a tray of dirty crockery. He cried out in warning, she caught at the tray, and together they steadied the wobbling china.

But Rita's bag had fallen from under her arm and skidded across the tiled corridor, spilling its contents. Darina came and took the tray from them, placing it safely on the kitchen table.

When she returned to the corridor, Nicholas and Rita were picking up the quantity of items the Irish writer seemed to find necessary to carry around with her. Several lipsticks, two notebooks, powder compact, mirror, three biros, a tiny bottle of Tabasco sauce, an empty pill bottle, wallet, purse, credit card case, Swiss knife, a pencil sharpener, book of stamps, driving licence and a small, furry toy.

"What an incredible amount of rubbish I manage to carry around," Rita clucked as each item was returned to the bag, "it's more than time I had a good sort-out." She jammed in the last few items, thanked them and returned to the refectory.

Nicholas was left with Darina. He followed her back into the kitchen, standing like an awkward stork as she started stacking the dishwasher. Finally she said, "What is it, Nicholas?"

"Ah, I just wanted to make sure you didn't misunderstand my concern for Miss Makepeace."

Darina stared at him. "You mean you want me to realise you are genuinely worried about her condition, not hoping her dead to save you from possibly embarrassing proceedings over Digby's book? Why should I even have thought that?"

He flushed. "I don't think any of you realise the harm a scandal like that could do the society."

Darina reached the end of her tether. "Have you not thought, Nicholas, it could show the society in a *good* light if you backed her claim, or at least gave it serious consideration? Now, if you'll excuse me, there is lunch to prepare. Frances will be here any minute and I want to get these dishes out of the way before she arrives."

She made a determined clatter with plates, deliberately turning her back on the silenced professor. When she turned round again, he had gone.

TWENTY

Darina worked with half her mind on Miss Makepeace struggling for life and half of it running over the curious aspects of her collapse.

Inspector Grant had seemed very concerned about the contents of the pill bottle and the possibility of an overdose. But in the end he had appeared to accept her condition with more ease than Darina found she could.

From what the doctor had said, even if Miss Makepeace had taken more pills after she had left her, they should not have had any serious effect. And if the countrywoman had decided to leave life and join her sister, Darina could not see her leaving a couple of pills in the bottle. But neither could she see her abandoning her struggle to achieve recognition for her book. Suicide, Darina would have said, had been a long way from her mind.

What did that leave? Heart attack? Darina had no experience of heart attacks, but surely victims did not look as peaceful as Miss Makepeace had that morning, and wouldn't the doctor have found some signs if that had been the case?

The effect of alcohol combined with the pill or pills? What had the doctor said: it could potentiate the effect of the drug? That must mean step it up.

What had Miss Makepeace drunk last night? Several glasses of wine and one of brandy. Was that enough to cause an otherwise healthy woman to lapse into a coma when combined with a sleeping pill or two? Particularly if she was used to consuming glasses of home-made wine most evenings.

As Darina turned over the possibilities in her mind, a picture of the hot milk and honey standing on the table in the hall whilst she was being questioned by the police came slowly into focus.

First, she pushed away the implications, then reluctantly forced herself to consider them.

Everyone in the bar had known of her intention to take it to Miss Makepeace, everyone had known of Miss Makepeace's intention to take a sleeping pill. And whilst Darina was with the police, any of the others had had the opportunity to slip something into the milk.

Then she thought that they could hardly have counted on having it presented to them, almost literally on a plate, like that. Had someone just seen it sitting there and taken a swift advantage of the opportunity? Did anyone have an alibi?

Rita, apparently, had seen Miss Makepeace was all right then gone to her room. Had her departure after the other woman been suspiciously swift?

Nicholas, he claimed, was walking in the garden, after brushing off Linda like a piece of lint from a dinner jacket. And she had dashed to her room. Had she stayed there?

Gray had gone to find a room in the annexe, with his dog, leaving Charles alone in the room they had shared. Again, there was nothing to prove either had not returned to the hall. Any of them could have added something to the milk.

And the reason why one of them should want to remove Miss Makepeace from the scene? Had it something to do with Digby's murder and the fact she was due to be interviewed by the police this morning? Or the fact that she had announced her intention of fighting for her rights to the book on pastry?

Only one person was really interested in her claims to the pastry book, and that was Nicholas. Darina remembered the story Gray had told her of poor Jameson and his overdose. Charles Childe had been right when he said Miss Makepeace's death would simplify things for Nicholas. Could he have decided to make sure no scandal would touch his precious society?

Or had Digby's murderer decided she was in possession of dangerous evidence? If so, it must be something to do with what she had seen when she looked over the banisters. Or had she placed a new interpretation on some detail Darina had seen and accepted at face value? Why, oh why, hadn't she questioned Miss Makepeace more closely, won her confidence and found out exactly what it was that was worrying her? It was all very well thinking the police would take care of the evidence, that it was no place of hers to go nosing around, but look what had happened!

When was it Miss Makepeace had looked over the banisters? Before or after Darina had gone downstairs?

Darina saw again the scene with the maddened dog, Charles sinking onto the bottom step, his hand dripping blood over the polished wood, Gray taking the dog off to the boiler room, then the arrival of the others. Nicholas in his cardigan pressing a handkerchief into her hand, Rita in her amazing red silk dressing gown with the golden dragon. And Linda nowhere to be seen.

That was what she had witnessed. But what did she know of what had happened before she arrived on the scene? Charles had come downstairs, Gray had entered the front door with Bracken off the leash and the dog had immediately attacked Charles. And that was it.

Darina scraped the remains of herb omelette and devilled kidneys off a serving dish and pondered. She added the scrap of evidence that had floated into her mind early that morning to the scene on the stairs. Then, all at once, the murder events fell neatly into place. She could see almost precisely what had happened.

The question remained, what to do now? Darina still had no proof, but did she have enough to go to the police, particularly in the light of Miss Makepeace's condition?

For a long time she stood with her hands in dirty washing-up water and rolled the problem around in her mind, collecting ideas like a cheese roulade nuts.

When Frances entered the kitchen a little later, she found Darina rolling out pastry.

"Ignore me," said the cook when asked what she was doing, "get on with the olio, I'll have finished this in a minute."

Frances trussed a large chicken then prepared various vegetables. As soon as Darina had finished with her pastry, she put a huge pot of stock on the stove and added the vegetables and seasonings. As it heated, she tied up a joint of beef. A small leg of lamb, a large garlic sausage and half a haunch of venison were also tied so that each could be suspended by its string.

When the stock came to the boil, the lamb and venison were added to the pot. After bubbles started gradually rising to the surface again, Darina covered the huge pot, and placed it in the slow oven of the Aga.

She gave Frances instructions to serve coffee then left the kitchen by the door opposite the boiler room and knocked on the door of the housekeeper's room. It was opened by a policeman.

"Will you be much longer in here?" She craned her neck to try and see the chalk outline on the floor.

"Just finished," he said cheerfully. "We're packing up here and moving on to see what other areas of the house can yield." He stood aside and invited her in.

Darina looked round the room. The typewriter was pushed back against the wall, and Digby's files and papers had gone. The books and knives, all covered with grey powder, were carelessly stacked beside the machine. Everywhere a myriad of fingerprints had been revealed by the powder, even the items on the dresser had been treated.

The policeman noticed Darina's look of surprise. "Can't afford to let anything escape our attention," he said, picking something up from the table. "We found this on the floor, reckoned it came from that spice box over there." He nodded towards the dresser.

Darina looked at the nutmeg in the palm of his hand. What an age it seemed since Digby had startled her into dropping the box, a different lifetime. The girl who had picked up the scattered contents had been a different person from the one who now looked at the hard, grained brown nut. "Did you think it might be a case of David and Goliath?" she said. "Sorry to disappoint you, I dropped the box on Friday night and I must have failed to pick that one up."

Darina could now see the position of the chalk outline. She considered its position in relation to the desk. Not all that far away. Not near enough to the central table for the murderer to have grabbed a knife and killed Digby without advancing towards him. But far enough away from the other table to suggest Digby had got up from the chair and was standing before being stabbed. She thought again of Digby's height and the entry point of the knife in his chest.

"Was there something you wanted, miss?" asked the policeman, looking at her curiously.

She realised she had been standing holding the nutmeg in silence for several minutes. She had not even realised she had taken it out of his hand.

"Sorry, nothing." She handed back the small nut and left the room thinking deeply.

Back in the kitchen, Darina joined Frances in working swiftly and efficiently to prepare the rest of the meal. But for once Darina's heart was not in her cooking. For once she wished something simpler had been chosen for the lunch. Instead of revelling in the quality of the ingredients and the whole-hearted extravagance of the effect they were creating, she felt embarrassed by the prodigality of the dish, the fact that only a fraction of what they were preparing would be eaten. What appetites they must have had in previous centuries. Or had an army of servants consumed the left-overs? It wasn't until Victorian times that recycling cold meats was developed into an art.

As she worked, she willed Deborah Makepeace to fight, to pull herself out of the ante-room to death, return to the living world. As her cold hands turned vegetables, she saw before her once again that morning's detached face and heard the laboured breathing. And through her mind ran the comfortable voice describing a life of hard physical labour and concentrated research.

Sergeant Pigram came into the kitchen. His normally pleasant air of quiet cheerfulness had vanished and he wore an expression of strained seriousness.

"The inspector wishes to see you, Miss Lisle," he said, holding open the door.

Darina's heart dropped. Without a word she left her preparations and went through.

Grant was sitting behind the writing desk making notes. He looked up as Darina entered and indicated the chair in front of him. There was a chill air of formality in the room. Darina sat, wishing she was back with the sergeant at the kitchen table.

"I'm sorry to have to tell you, Miss Lisle, that Miss Makepeace died a short while ago."

Darina closed her eyes and a deep, burning anger lit inside her. An anger far more intense than any she had felt at Digby's death. The quiet countrywoman had done no one harm and Nicholas's precious society had first stage-managed the theft of her life's work and then deprived her of life itself.

She looked at Grant. "I'm sorry," she said levelly.

"I would like you to repeat to me the story you told this morning."

"About the milk?"

"About the milk, yes."

With a sense of foreboding, Darina slowly ran through the details again.

"So Miss Makepeace said the drink tasted odd?" the inspector asked quietly when she had finished.

"It was the honey, it was from firs and had a distinctly resinous flavour. That was why I took the biscuits as well, in case she didn't like the taste."

"In case she didn't like the taste," repeated Grant.

"You think there was something else in the drink?" challenged Darina.

He refused to answer the question directly. "What happened to the mug and saucepan afterwards, Miss Lisle?"

"I washed up the saucepan. The mug went into the dishwasher, which I switched on before going to bed."

"But it was only half full," interjected William.

"I wanted it empty for the morning, you didn't question my action at the time." Darina was appalled to hear how defensive she sounded. "I realise what you are getting at, I'm not stupid. But do you realise that whilst you were questioning me in here about Digby's plagiarism, that mug of milk was standing on the table in the hall? Anyone could have slipped something in it."

"We are talking about you and your opportunities," Grant said smoothly.

"And what would have been my motive?"

"I can think of several. You told Sergeant Pigram there was something Miss Makepeace was worried about that she was going to tell us this morning. It is more than possible that she had a clue to the murder that could incriminate you, perhaps one she didn't recognise? It would be very much in your interest to ensure she was never questioned.

"Then there is the question of this book on pastry. It forms part of the estate Mr. Cary was free to leave you. If Miss Makepeace intended to fight her claim, your inheritance could be substantially reduced, both by legal costs and possible loss of revenue."

"If I had just murdered Miss Makepeace, I would hardly have told the police she had something she was anxious to tell them next morning. And I told her she should press her claim to the book, I even suggested that it might be possible to prove it," protested Darina.

"You've just said yourself you are not stupid. Both moves could have been calculated to divert any suspicion from yourself."

"This is totally preposterous. Where am I supposed to have got hold of the sleeping pills, or whatever else I'm supposed to have put in that milk?"

"You didn't bring any with you?" Grant's voice was silky smooth and Darina suddenly hesitated from uttering the denial that sprang to her lips. From his pocket he drew a little plastic bag and placed it in front of her on the table. "Recognise these?"

Inside the sachet was a little brown bottle. On the label was Darina's name. Inside an odd tablet could just be seen. She looked at it with a sinking heart.

"Yes," she said without emotion, "that is mine. I'd forgotten it was in my toilet bag. They were prescribed for me over a year ago, you can see the date on the bottle. It was after my cousin's wife died. I had spent most of the last week of her life with her and the doctor insisted I take them for a night or two to get some proper sleep. I went straight home to my mother after the funeral and I must have left them in the bag. I don't think I took more than one or two."

"There's only one left in the bottle," said Grant.

Darina tried to think. "He didn't give me many, he said they were very strong—I know they zonked me out, I could hardly function the following day. I can't remember exactly how many there were. I think my mother asked if she could have some." It sounded horribly lame and Darina knew better than to press the point. She could think of nothing else to say.

Grant let the little bottle in its protective covering drop to the table. He reached behind him and brought forward another, much larger bag and placed it in front of Darina.

"I suppose you know nothing of these?"

Darina looked at the bag in amazement. "My rubber gloves! I wondered what had happened to those, I couldn't find them yesterday morning—where were they?"

"In the plant pot in the hall, stuffed between the elephant container and the aspidistra." He manipulated the plastic bag to display one finger of the gloves. "It looks as if there is blood here. I have no doubt that analysis will show it is Cary's. They must have been used by the murderer when wiping the knife and door handle clean of prints."

Darina forgot her predicament for a moment as another little piece of jigsaw slipped into place. She looked across at Grant.

"Anybody could have taken those from the kitchen, just as anybody could have doctored that milk in the hall. If I had been the murderer, I'd have returned the gloves to the kitchen, soaked them in the washing-up bowl. And if I'd wanted to kill Miss Makepeace"— for a moment bile rose in her throat, but she swallowed resolutely and continued—"don't you think I'd have chosen a method that didn't point quite so obviously to me? And wasn't it I who called for the doctor when I found her?"

"Ah yes, both victims were found by you, weren't they, Miss Lisle? Do you know how often it is the murderer who discovers the body? It is quite the most suspicious action you could have undertaken."

"Well, I'm sorry, next time I find a body I will make sure nobody knows." Darina was so angry at his stupidity she hardly knew what she was saying. She took a deep breath and thought before she spoke again, choosing her words with care. "You are completely mistaken and you have no proof."

"Except these." Grant lifted up the bag containing the pill bottle. "If the analysis of Miss Makepeace's stomach contents finds pills like these killed her, I'm afraid you are going to have to answer many more questions, Miss Lisle. Bill, see these and the gloves are sent to the lab." He passed the two plastic envelopes over to the sergeant, who took them out of the room without a glance at Darina. She found that the most sinister aspect of the whole interview.

She waited to be arrested.

"You are free to go and get on with lunch, Miss Lisle, but I advise you not to attempt to leave the grounds."

Surprised, she said, "Aren't you worried I'll poison the food and do you all in?"

"Come now, Miss Lisle, *all* of us?"

She turned, furious, and left the room.

Outside she almost ran into William Pigram on his way back from the front door. "Steady," he said, catching her by the shoulders.

She wrenched herself away. "You can keep your hands off me for a little while at least, the inspector hasn't decided to arrest me yet," she flung at him. "But I'm sure you sent those pills off by the fastest possible carrier to make sure it's not long delayed."

She stood breathing quickly, outrage filling every crevice of her body.

"It's one of his ways," said William quietly, "to get under the skin of suspects and make them angry. He says that's when the guilty make mistakes."

"Oh, is it?" Darina spat the words at him. "Then I suggest you join us for lunch and see some real action."

William grew very still. "What are you getting at?"

"Come to lunch," repeated Darina.

"If you've got any evidence, you must tell us."

Evidence, that was the trouble, she hadn't any evidence, only an elegantly simple theory based on one statement that could easily be denied.

"Come to lunch," she reiterated.

"Don't be childish!" He saw immediately he had made a fatal mistake. "I mean, don't think we aren't considering every other possibility. All the other bedrooms are being checked for sleeping pills right now."

"Bill!" came a sharp voice. He groaned. Grant was standing in the door of the incident room, his face a thundercloud.

Darina escaped swiftly through the refectory door.

TWENTY-ONE

In the kitchen, all was ready for lunch. Darina went to the bar to call the symposiasts. Behind the incident room door she could hear Grant laying down the law. She smiled grimly to herself; the law in the shape of one long, lean sergeant could do with a little chastening. As for Grant, he could receive a surprise. Then her spirits dropped: what if her plan failed? What if the murderer realised what her intention was and refused to be drawn? Would she have ruined any chance the police might have to force a confession? For a moment she considered going back, knocking at the incident room door and telling them all her suspicions.

Then she thought of Grant's chilly manner, the way he had marshalled his evidence against her. Wouldn't he consider any such story as she could muster now merely a vain attempt to deflect suspicion from herself? No, she must continue with her plan. If it succeeded, the murderer would be plain for all to see.

She entered the bar. No one noticed her at first. There seemed to be a conference going on. Linda had her clipboard in action. "OK," she said, writing busily, "we've got Nicholas on the society, Rita on Digby as cookery writer, Charles on the television side. Gray, what can you contribute?"

Gray rose irritably, went to the bar and poured himself a whisky. Judging from the number of glasses around, everyone had been drinking freely. "You can leave me out of the whole operation, unless you want me to blow the reputation of your precious Digby Cary sky-high. How you can bring yourself to speak warmly of the man who so slaughtered your restaurant is beyond me," he said scornfully to Charles Childe, lounging with careful ease in an armchair.

Charles looked benignly back at the angry man. "Speak no ill of the dead, you know, and with luck that review will never see the light of day."

Gray made an exasperated noise and then noticed Darina. "Ah, the one sensible person connected with this whole terrible weekend. Can I get you a drink, Darina?"

She shook her head, looking at him regretfully. She'd been so attracted to the shaggy figure that first night. Now she saw a sad and bitter man who had lacked the strength and understanding to achieve either his personal or his professional dream and had allowed the knowledge to infect his whole character. He would never write his best-seller. Once, she might have found a purpose in filling his life with love and gradually injecting him with renewed confidence. Not now.

"I'm making the final arrangements for the programme on Digby," said Linda, "you must make a contribution." She waited expectantly.

Darina took a step towards her then came to a full stop. This whole thing was nonsense. What did any of them understand of Digby's life, what could they show of Digby as he really was? Would the fact that because of him an innocent woman lay dead in a lonely hospital bed disturb them? Didn't they realise a murderer was one of their company?

"If you like," she said, "I would be willing to say something of Digby as a cook. A cook who understood food, its taste and treatment, better than anyone else I know. If he'd wanted, he could have been a great chef. Some of his early recipes were wonderful: simple, respecting the flavour of the main ingredient but complementing it in unexpected ways. He could serve you carrot and make you realise you had never really appreciated carrot before." She stopped, aware her audience was not really interested.

"Digby as carrot chef! It's not how I'll remember him but perhaps we can work that in somewhere." Linda made a note on her board.

"Lunch is ready," announced Darina abruptly, turning and leaving the room without further ceremony. What did any of them understand about food? What they wanted was the excitement factor; Digby as a great cookery writer, as television star, as maker and breaker of restaurants. She bet Charles's restaurant went in for radish flowers.

Rita caught her up as she entered the hall. "Darina, darling girl,

I've the most heavenly bit of news." Her eyes were bright and a flush highlighted her cheekbones. Ten years seemed to have dropped from her age. "I finally managed to reach Russell Thomas on the phone. Russell Thomas," she repeated as Darina looked at her blankly, "sure and isn't he only the best features editor in Fleet Street, oh, excuse me, on the Isle of Dogs. Well, and hasn't the dear man said I can take over Digby's weekly column! On a temporary basis," she hastily added, "until, he says, they can 'assess the situation.' But sure they'll have decided by then I can keep the job. It's only the break I've been wanting these last five long years. A chance to show I'm up there with the rest of them. Isn't he just the darling man? And who would have thought it would be Digby who'd give me the opportunity."

Darina had never heard Rita so Irish before. Excitement seemed to fizz out of her like gas from a newly opened tonic bottle. Her life had been given new purpose and meaning. Even beyond the grave Digby had the power to affect others' lives.

Would he be amused at this development? Find it ironic? Or see it as a final act of revenge? Had he ever really considered the effect he could have on the lives of others? And at the end, had he regretted not using the compassion that could have saved his life?

Darina murmured something to Rita and continued on into the kitchen, where Frances had matters firmly in hand.

Lunch started badly. Inspector Grant and Sergeant Pigram had appeared just as the symposiasts were sitting down. They went to the extra places Darina had laid and Grant stood in the manner of a cleric waiting to say grace. There was an awkward shuffle as those who had sat half rose, not sure what was to happen.

"Please sit down," he said pleasantly. More shuffle as everyone now sat, William Pigram unobtrusively placing a notebook and pencil beside his plate.

"I regret to announce," Grant started when they were settled, "that Miss Makepeace died in hospital a short while ago. We are treating her death as murder." On which note he, too, sat.

There was a shocked silence. Then Nicholas cleared his throat. "Why murder, Inspector? I understood she had taken an overdose of sleeping pills."

Grant's eyes narrowed. "Did you, sir? What gave you that impression?"

Nicholas cleared his throat again, the action now overtly nervous, his Adam's apple working convulsively. His eyes shifted from the inspector's and darted looks round the table. "Why, I don't know, I assumed, that is, someone said—Darina, wasn't it you, didn't you find Miss Makepeace?"

In the act of placing a huge plate of carved meats in the middle of the table, Darina hesitated. What had she said when giving the news of Miss Makepeace's condition? Surely nothing about any sleeping pills? She took a moment positioning the plate with its carefully arranged burden of meats garnished with vegetables, egg and melted butter.

"I'm not sure," she answered finally, standing aside to let Frances serve the plates.

Linda already had a vegetable casserole in front of her. She inserted a fork daintily as the others started to lean forward and help themselves from the olio. A very slight pinkness stained her cheekbones. "It was something I gathered from the conversation after Darina asked for the doctor to be called," she murmured.

The glance Nicholas gave her was comically grateful. He sat back with the air of one who has been grievously misjudged. "Of course, that was it! But, Inspector, you still have not told us why you think Miss Makepeace was murdered."

But the inspector was looking keenly at Linda. "Wasn't it rather a conclusion that you drew yourself, Miss Stainmore? One that you could be said to have been keen to implant in our minds?"

She stared back at him, poise firmly in place. "What are you suggesting, Inspector?"

"I would just like to know what you took on Friday night that caused you to sleep so soundly you never heard Mr. Wyndham's dog attack Mr. Childe."

Linda rose gracefully. "This is hardly the place to continue this morning's interview, Inspector, and I dislike your tone. I have already told you I take herbal draughts. I think I will leave you."

"Sit down!" Grant's tone was hardly raised from its normal level but Linda abruptly collapsed back into her place. Nicholas put his hand on hers.

Grant looked round the table. "Understand," he said in his pleasantly low-key manner, "no one leaves this room except Miss Lisle, who may go to the kitchen. All your rooms are being searched. Someone round this table murdered Miss Makepeace. That someone almost certainly also murdered Mr. Cary and I intend to find out who before the end of the afternoon."

There was stunned silence.

"You've hardly been very successful with your murder investigation so far." Charles reached across for an artichoke bottom and another slice of chicken, shooting a sly glance at the inspector, his face the picture of innocence.

"Now that we have two murders, there are double the number of mistakes for us to identify," Grant said, his manner completely composed.

If Grant had intended to unsettle his suspects, success was his. For a moment there was uneasy silence. Slices of the various meats were toyed with, cauliflower florets and turned turnips pushed around plates, then Gray put down his fork and said abruptly, "I can understand why anyone would want to murder Digby Cary, global spring-cleaning could not have made the world a fresher place, but why Miss Makepeace?" His hair shaggier than ever, he looked the picture of a naïve academic.

"Don't you, sir?" Grant was pleasant but pointed.

Gray laced his hands across the top of his plate and gazed at the inspector, a look of dawning comprehension rising on his face, but Rita was quicker. "Sure, the dear man is meaning she must have known something."

Grant inclined his head in her direction. "I'm grateful to you, Ms. Moore."

"But what could she have known?" Nicholas sounded genuinely bewildered. "I thought she was asleep when Digby was killed— whenever that was," he added hastily.

"Miss Lisle has repeated to us a conversation with Miss Makepeace during which she told her she'd seen something of the incident with the dog that puzzled her. She was to go through the event with us this morning. Exactly what it was, Miss Lisle claims she didn't say." All eyes became fixed on Darina. She continued trying to eat a quail.

"You were all there," the inspector went on smoothly, "all except Miss Stainmore, who says she was fast asleep under the influence of a herbal draught." Subtle doubt laced his voice. "Miss Makepeace was an unusual woman of some intelligence. There is no doubt in my mind that something, some part of that scene struck her as odd, so odd that eventually she realised its significance. Unfortunately, before she could let us know what it was, she was murdered."

The only person round the table who showed any appetite for the olio was William Pigram. He had consumed a good portion of each of the meats and of the accompaniments and was now helping himself to more lamb with every appearance of deep enjoyment. Darina wondered how many similar scenes he had attended. Was he really as unconcerned as he seemed? As if aware of her scrutiny, the silvery grey eyes slid a look in her direction and she realised he was as alert as any gun-dog waiting for the fall of a pheasant.

"So, once again Digby is behind the whole debacle." Nicholas was back to his peevish self.

"Ah yes, Professor, you were locked in rivalry with the deceased over the society, weren't you?"

Nicholas blustered but Grant was remorseless. "As you were with another academic at one time, I believe? Who died of an overdose of sleeping pills?"

The colour drained out of the professor's face as completely as blood from a kosher-killed chicken. He stared at Grant as though Tutankhamen had shed his swaddling layers and risen before him.

Then he looked straight at Gray. "You, you told them. You snivelling failure of an historian, you're just jealous of someone else's success."

Gray flushed but before he could attempt a response there was a strangled sound from Linda. She raised a hand towards Nicholas, then took it away again. He looked at her with anguish in his eyes but she refused to meet his gaze, the porcelain perfection of her face under its cap of shining black hair as set as that of a Japanese Noh performer.

Lunch was not following the course Darina had planned at all. She looked at Grant. He was calmly surveying the table, allowing the tensions to stimulate whatever disclosures they might. It was as though he believed proof of the murderer's identity would appear without further effort on his part.

The time had come, she thought, to give matters a little prod of her own.

"Nicholas," she said into the silence that had lengthened alarmingly. Grant made an almost imperceptible gesture of annoyance. Her intervention had released the tension and the professor turned to her like a drowning man turning his face towards an approaching lifeboat. "Did you say something about wanting my recipes so you could have them typed out for the symposiasts?"

Charles Childe's attention was caught. "Recipes?"

Nicholas passed his hand over his face, rubbing his eyes. "Recipes," he repeated, looking at Darina. "Recipes?" Comprehension arrived. "Of course, recipes." Something like his old spirit reanimated him. "That's right! I thought it would be an excellent idea to circulate them among the symposiasts, hopefully together with a date for the rescheduled weekend."

Charles looked delighted.

"Now you won't have to pay for them," Darina murmured to him as she started clearing away empty plates.

"I may still want advice on how they should be cooked," he said, cocking his head on one side and sneaking her a glance from under his long lashes. Of them all, he seemed least affected by the news of Miss Makepeace's death and the accusation of murder from the inspector. "I must know how many pots you had to use to produce this magnificent assembly, and the exact order you added all the different ingredients." He poked at a carrot amongst the debris of the dish.

"I'll be delighted," she said. "I could prepare step by step instructions for you." She took a pile of crockery behind the screen then came back for more. "What were the dishes you thought you could be interested in?" Rita shot her an agonised look of despair as Charles took a deep breath and launched himself happily into speech with a dissertation on the hopes and aims he had for the dishes that were to launch Bon Appetit into a new era.

Darina picked up the last of the olio and disappeared off to the kitchen, leaving him in full flow. She picked up a large tart and told Frances to bring plates.

Charles was still holding forth as they returned to the dining room. Eyes were glazed. Gray was arranging cutlery and pepper pots in a pattern on the table. Nicholas had his gaze fixed on Linda, who sat with eyes downcast, hands clasped in her lap. The two policemen were listening to the restaurateur with horrified fascination. They hadn't been present at the dinner the previous evening to hear his similar performance.

Rita looked up reproachfully as the two girls entered.

"Wasn't that one of the dishes you were interested in?" Darina said as she placed the tart on the table in front of Charles.

He studied the pastry with a satisfied smirk. "Yes, indeed, I was fascinated to know exactly how you had cut the pastry. The way it's folded back, so effective."

"So it *was* this tart you were referring to last night," said Darina, watching him. Out of the corner of her eye she could see William Pigram lean forward slightly to get a better view of the dish.

Nicholas transferred his gaze from Linda to the table then looked puzzled. "I don't understand," he said. "When did you produce this before, Darina?"

"Yes," she said softly, still looking at Charles, "when was it you saw Robert May's tart, cut, you may like to know, to resemble virginal keys?"

TWENTY-TWO

If a poisonous snake had suddenly lifted its head out of the tart, Charles could not have frozen more still. His eyes darted from side to side, his tongue nervously licked his lips. The two policemen sat very quietly but Rita leaned forward. "Sure and it's a beautiful effect but you don't expect us to eat this after that olio, Darina? If I remember aright, it's hardly pudding material."

William Pigram, sitting next to her, put a hand on her arm. She looked at him in surprise; he gave her a warning glance then returned his attention to the man sitting rigidly on the other side of the table.

Charles gave a little shake of his head. "It's too difficult to remember exactly when you produced everything." He made a painful attempt to smile lightly. "Wasn't it one of the tarts we had at that first meal?"

"No," said Darina softly, never taking her eyes from him, "it should have appeared at lunch yesterday but the dog ate it some time during Friday night. The only time you could have seen it was if you were in the kitchen after I went to bed at quarter to twelve, well after you heard Rita with Digby."

Grant's attention was now also fixed on Charles Childe.

He sat, his face white, his eyes flicking round the faces turned towards him. Suddenly he started trembling violently. "He made me do it," he whimpered, staring at Darina, his eyes caught by hers. She remained standing in front of the table, drawn up to her full height, shoulders back, her face implacable.

"The things he said. And I'd only gone to ask him if he'd written the review of Bon Appetit yet. It was so important, you see." He looked pleadingly at her. "We really needed a good review. It's been such a struggle to establish ourselves, nobody realises how strong the

competition is and Wandsworth, though *the* 'in' place, *is* quite a way
from the West End. We haven't been covering our costs for some
time. Digby Cary could have changed all that." He sounded deeply
aggrieved. "A good review from Mr. Emperor of Restaurant Critics
could have put us on the map.

"When he came into Bon Appetit that night I thought everything
might be about to change. He called me his 'dear Charles.' " Darina
flinched as Digby's voice suddenly filled the room, the ringing tones
coming oddly from the small man opposite her. Further down the
table, she noticed William was quietly taking notes.

"I chatted him up, made sure he had all the best items; that
chicken stuffed with walnuts, apricots, celery and green peppers
with the cranberry sauce was just divine, everyone said so. And my
trifle, that he said resembled a badly decorated Christmas tree, really
is out of this world and looks so pretty with the gold and silver
dragées mingling with glacé cherries and angelica. Mind you, I'm
surprised he noticed the food at all, the attention he was lavishing on
his companion. Talk about Christmas baubles, her place was on top
of the tree."

He looked round the table. The terrified man had gone and the
actor was now in complete control, playing to the most fascinated
audience of his career.

"I thought if I could nobble him at this weekend, I could make
sure we got a reasonable review. I should have known better. We'd
started out so well with that TV series, such an attractive man I
thought when we first met, and he really seemed to like me. At one
stage I even thought . . . but when I made the tiniest little move
towards him, he switched off, just like that. You'd have thought I'd
suggested we steal the crown jewels. Nothing I could do was right
after that. He took every opportunity he could to do me down and I
know it was he who killed the idea of a third series.

"And he must have poisoned the director against me because he
wouldn't even consider a wonderful idea I came up with for a completely different sort of programme with just me. And, no matter
what any smarty-pants producer says"—he shot Linda a malevolent
glance—"it was Digby Cary who took away my column. My foodie
diary was good, all my friends said so." He fell silent, full of the
catalogue of Digby's sins against him.

"So you decided to tackle him after Rita had finished," suggested Darina quietly, slipping into her seat opposite him. "What did you do, listen outside the door, then hide in the boiler room so she wouldn't see you as she left?"

His face brightened at this evidence of an intelligent audience. "Yes, exactly. When I'd heard him calm down after her tirade—what a performance you gave, Rita, you said so many things I'd have liked to—I thought everything would be all right. And when I first went in, it was. He smiled at me, said at last someone he didn't need to feel guilty about. I thought he meant he'd given us a good review, then he handed me the article and said would I like to read it before he sent it off." Charles's eyes opened wide, the shock of the moment vividly before him. "I couldn't believe it! All those *terrible* things he said about us. And he stood there and laughed at me." Charles closed his eyes for a moment.

"That article would have finished us." He looked straight at Darina. "I'd have been bankrupt, everything lost. I really only wanted to give him a fright. There were all those knives on the table. I grabbed one, thrust the article back at him and told him unless he altered it, made it a good review, I'd stick the knife into him. He didn't even stop laughing. He just put the article back on his desk and said I'd better put it down before I cut myself! If only he hadn't laughed like that! As though I was a nothing, a fly he could brush away with one flick of his hand!" Charles's eyes became unfocussed, he was back in the housekeeper's room.

"If he hadn't laughed, I'd have put the knife back. But he just stood there, laughing, and all he'd done to me surged up like, like awful vomit." He almost gagged on the word. "I took a step towards him, holding out the knife as though I was going to stab him. I wanted to, oh how I wanted to, but I wouldn't have really, only my foot stepped on something and I slipped. I must have flung up my hand as I stumbled because the next thing I knew was Digby had given an amazing little grunt and was sort of collapsed on me.

"I hadn't even realised the knife had gone in, it slipped through his ribs so easily! I let the handle go and stepped back and he just sank down on the floor." His voice dwindled to a whisper then died away altogether.

No one moved, not a word was said and after a moment Charles continued, by now talking to Darina alone. Everyone else could have vanished for all the notice he took of them.

"I could see he was dead. I never realised how horribly obvious death can be before. First I thought I must tell someone. Then I realised that no one knew I'd done it. I could take the article and my restaurant would be safe. There was hardly any blood, just a little on my cuff, but I knew I had to remove my fingerprints. So I went into the kitchen, it was dark so I reckoned you'd finished. I found a pair of rubber gloves and a cloth. Then I saw the tart.

"I was so calm, it was just like being in a play, it seemed quite natural to admire the pastry, the way you'd made that pattern. I thought I must try and do something like it for the restaurant." He gave a bleak little laugh. "I didn't realise that no one else would have seen it.

"I wiped my fingerprints off everything, and how I got to that knife I'll never know, he was so heavy. I had to sort of crawl under the body, but I did it. Then I took the article, it never occurred to me to look for a copy, turned off all the lights and left. But when I reached the hall, I found I'd still got the rubber gloves on. I couldn't take them upstairs, Mr. High and Mighty Wyndham would have thought them not quite the wear for a bedroom"—the light voice mimicked a refined accent—"so I stuffed them into the elephant pot, all those lovely bulges in the side held them beautifully.

"Then I came all over queer. It was the shock, I suppose. I mean, you don't kill someone every day, do you? I just couldn't get beyond the first step, I had to sit on the stair. I think I groaned. Then, as I dragged myself up again, I heard a little gasp from upstairs. I looked up and thought I saw someone drawing back but I couldn't be sure, and that's when that vicious brute was let loose on me!" He looked at Gray with hatred in his eyes.

"I never did like dogs!" He cradled the wounded hand with his good one. He seemed to have run out of steam rather than finished making a statement.

"When did you decide Miss Makepeace had to be removed?" asked Grant, his face as impassive as it had been throughout the actor's recital.

Charles hesitated, a look of cunning on his face, then, "That's something you can't lay at my door," he said.

There was a knock, then a policeman entered holding a small plastic bag identical to the one that had contained Darina's bottle of sleeping pills.

The inspector got up and went across to him. There was a whispered conversation. Grant came back and stood looking at Charles, the plastic bag in his hand. "This has been found stuck in the U-bend of the toilet in your bathroom. I think the time has come to take an official statement."

TWENTY-THREE

"Charles Childe is now being held by the police and this extraordinary weekend can finally come to a close.

"For a nerve-racking thirty-six hours, those of us who slept in the main abbey building, including myself, have been under suspicion of murder, and one of us has died because of what she knew. What had been intended as a weekend studying our cooking heritage has been a time fraught with tension and even"—the voice sank to a dramatic whisper—"fear! as we wondered who amongst us was a murderer and whether he would strike again." There was the briefest of pauses then the voice became briskly matter-of-fact. "This is Linda Stainmore at the Abbey Conference Centre for Bristol TV."

The picture changed from the outside of the abbey, with Linda svelte in her suède jeans, and returned to the studio. The urbane announcer said, "Linda Stainmore's memorial programme to Digby Cary will be shown on this channel tomorrow night at ten-thirty."

Darina clicked off the picture and looked at Frances. They were sitting in the bar, in front of a small television set. The clearing-up had all been done, the others had left.

After the two policemen had taken Charles Childe off to the incident room, the symposiasts sat in shocked silence. It even took Linda a moment to pull herself together and go in search of her camera crew. Then all had been feverish activity as she recorded quick pieces on Digby with those she hadn't managed to catch earlier.

Only Darina refused to take part in what she regarded as a hollow charade. She and Frances removed the dirty dishes and looked at the uneaten desserts. Elaborate jellies, with shapes of one colour swimming palely through moulds of another, seemed to have lost their sparkle and a Sussex pond pudding sagged drunkenly in its bowl, golden buttery liquid spilling out of the resplendent suet crust. Food had finally lost its appeal. Darina put the dishes carefully on one side; maybe the police would be grateful for them later.

Whilst Linda was recording her wrap-up piece at the front door, excited symposiasts watching in a group at the side, Grant had emerged with a sober and frightened-looking Charles Childe, his arm no longer carried in a sling, and bundled him unceremoniously into a police car. Darina, who had brought out a pot of tea for the television technicians, watched the car draw away. She found it difficult to identify the mixture of emotions that swirled through her as she stood back from the rush of the TV crew to capture the drama of the departure.

Relief was easy enough to recognise. Not only the relief that she herself was no longer under suspicion but also that Digby's murder had been solved. No longer need the gargantuan figure of her cousin loom over her, the shade had been laid to rest.

But alongside the relief was unease. As William Pigram turned back from seeing off his chief and the murderer, she put out a hand and stopped him. Before she could say anything, Linda was there, microphone at the ready, her cameraman, puffing slightly from his chase after the car, right behind.

"I'm sorry," said the detective sergeant, "I'll only say something if you send your camera away." He stood patiently whilst Linda weighed up her chances of persuading him otherwise, finally signalling to the technician to stand down. She then waited expectantly.

William backed slightly away from the press of interest as the others drew closer, and rubbed his eyes. With a slight shock, Darina realised he looked as tired as she felt. Somehow she'd been thinking of the police as automatons, machines programmed to investigate, assess and act without the need for the rest and sustenance that others required to keep going.

Briefly he told them Charles had admitted to murdering Miss Makepeace and that he was now to be charged with both killings. "I have to go down to the station now, I'll be back later," he finished, looking at Darina.

"In case I've managed to clear up and leave before then, I'll wish you luck for the future," she said coldly, unexpectedly put out by the fact he wouldn't talk to her now. His eyes held hers for a moment, then he nodded briefly and went off to collect a file of papers before driving away.

Darina disappeared back to the kitchen. She washed and dried, stacked and stored like a whirlwind. "What's the hurry?" asked Frances as she came back with the tray of used tea things. She watched Darina fill cardboard boxes with unused food. "Have you a date or something?"

"Don't you want to be out of here as soon as you can?" ground out Darina as she stuffed left-over vegetables into a plastic bag.

Frances gave her a quick look then began to help.

Their efforts were constantly interrupted by people coming to say goodbye.

The TV technicians were first, full of thanks for all the food. Linda had apparently already left. Then came Rita, her red hair aflame, her freckled face alight with excitement. She was full of plans for the columns Digby's editor had commissioned her to do. "And we must meet in London, Darina, darling. Well, there's Digby's funeral for one. You will let me know when and where? Here's my address." She pressed a card into Darina's hand and went out.

The funeral! With a sinking heart, Darina realised there was only her to arrange for Digby's last rites.

"I wondered . . ." Gray had entered the kitchen with Bracken on a lead. His eyes were shy but determined. "I wondered," he repeated, coming towards the table, now covered with boxes of hastily packed food, "if there was any way I could help. I mean, with tidying up after your cousin's death, funeral arrangements and so forth."

Darina's hands paused in their activities. She looked at the shaggy man in surprise. A change seemed to have come over him. His shoulders were straighter, the beard combed.

"It's very kind of you but I think I can manage." Now why had she refused his offer, just when the whole business of handling undertakers and memorial services had loomed so distastefully? "But I am sure there will be a lot of sorting out over the trust fund and the house. The contents, so much of the furniture must have been Sarah's and should go to you."

He looked embarrassed. "I know she had one or two Knapp family heirlooms but otherwise I am sure it should all be yours." He fiddled with the lead of the dog. Bracken, for once, was standing quietly at his side, giving no more than the odd sniff to the food on the table.

"I'm afraid you won't have got much information for your book," said Darina finally, wondering why he was still hanging around.

"Oh, that." He looked up, a new purpose shining out of his eyes. "I've decided to discard the whole thing. Never was my style. No, Sarah's trust fund means I can try and return to the academic world, go back to what I should have been doing from the start, researching small areas of limited interest; limited, that is, to chaps like me." He smiled ruefully. "I'll leave popular success to others." He picked up a tiny grater and flipped its little lid, looking at the half of a nutmeg it contained with detached interest. "I was wondering whether you'd like to come up to Dorrington some time, we've got some interesting household account books you might like to see?"

The brown eyes dragged themselves up to look at Darina. They were like Bracken's, pleading for affection, for attention, for some sign he held a place of importance in someone's life.

No, Darina said to herself, I'm not the right person for you, you mustn't waste time on me. Then she summoned up a smile. "It would be lovely," she said, knowing she was being a coward, "as soon as I have a little time to spare."

He brightened. "I'll be in touch and do let me know if you change your mind and would like some help over the next few days." Bracken came forward and licked her hand and she gave him a last caress before he left the kitchen with his master.

Another one Digby's death had benefited, and not only materially, mused Darina as she returned to her clearing-up operation.

A few minutes later Nicholas entered the kitchen.

"Darina, my dear, what can I say to thank you for all your efforts this weekend? I haven't been able to sort out possible new symposium dates yet but I will be in touch soon to make sure you will be free. Then your cooking will receive its due appreciation."

The last thing Darina wanted at that moment was to think about repeating her culinary activities of the past two days. She muttered something non-committal but Nicholas wasn't really listening.

"Amazing chap, that Childe, killing Digby, carrying on as though nothing had happened, then committing another murder. Poor Miss Makepeace," he finished perfunctorily before asking Darina for the recipes she'd used for the weekend. "I'll get them copied out and circulated. Not forgetting you, of course," he chuckled happily. "Can't forget the cook! Now, I must go and collect my bag, I'm meeting Linda at the TV station after she has edited her piece for the local news this evening. We're going out to dinner to celebrate the successful conclusion to this terrible weekend." He darted out of the kitchen with a quick nod in the direction of Frances.

Another who seemed so much more relaxed. Was Digby's epitaph to be the peace he'd brought to so many lives by his leaving?

After Nicholas had gone, all was quiet and she and Frances could finish stripping the kitchen of all their ingredients and equipment and load up Darina's estate car.

She looked at the amount of unconsumed meat in her large cool-boxes and sighed. How the weekend's invoicing was to be worked out, she had no idea. More problems. She pushed them aside and looked at her watch. "Do you want to see Linda's piece go out?" she asked Frances. "It's just about time."

"And I thought you were so keen to get off!" replied her assistant with a twinkle as she followed Darina through to the bar.

Darina poured them both a glass of wine and switched on the television, collapsing into a chair with a sigh as they settled to watch the programme.

"Still here?" It was William Pigram, looming tall in the bar door-way as Darina and Frances picked up their empty glasses and the television screen faded to a bright dot.

"I'll take these," said Frances, removing the wine glass from Darina's hand. "I'll give them a quick rinse downstairs and then be off, I've got to get back to town. Contact you in the morning." She left swiftly with a grin at the policeman. He sank into an armchair.

"At last, I thought we'd never be done with the formalities." He stretched out his long legs, looking relaxed and at ease. "You managed to flush out our murderer for us, didn't you, just as you said you would." He smiled at her ruefully. "I've never seen poor Grant so taken aback."

"He didn't show it!"

"Only to those who know him as well as I do."

"But it was only a matter of time before you found the pill bottle and identified Charles as the murderer anyway." Darina perched herself on a bar stool, not nearly so at ease.

"Maybe, but we'd probably have had a job to get him to confess and without that it would have been a hard slog building up the circumstantial evidence. Wyndham could have taken the pills and doctored the milk. Or someone else gone into his bedroom—unlikely, I know, but Childe could have protested his innocence quite effectively, there were no prints on the bottle. You may keep your moment of triumph, you deserve it!"

A companionable silence fell. Then William stirred himself. "I could do with a glass of wine. How about you?"

Darina allowed him to pour them both some dry white wine and watched him settle once again into the comfortable chair. She kept to her bar stool, feeling it somehow gave her a slight advantage, though why she should need one was a question she couldn't answer.

"Did Charles tell you exactly how he'd doctored the milk?"

"Crushed the tablets he'd got from the hospital on Friday night with the spoon you'd so thoughtfully provided for tea-making and slipped them into the mug whilst it was sitting on the table in the hall. Apparently he thought he would have to distract your attention in the kitchen. It seemed to him the gods were on his side when he saw it sitting there, left for anyone to help themselves to!"

"He can't have been thinking very straight, surely I would have remembered him 'distracting my attention'?"

"Ah, he didn't think Miss Makepeace's death would ever be identified as murder. Straight case of overdose of sleeping pills, he reckoned, if in fact they did kill her; he was by no means sure there would be enough. But if she survived, he hoped she would not be in any state to remember exactly what she'd seen over the banisters. And even if murder was suspected, he was confident there wouldn't be any evidence against him. He'd washed up the saucer and spoon and flushed the bottle, as he thought, down the loo. It never occurred to him we might search the drains or that eventually we would have checked on the medication he'd been given by the hospital and asked what had happened to it.

"You have to remember our Charles is not the brainiest of people. Low cunning is what has brought him through life so far. And he has a desperate need for recognition and applause. Once he'd brought himself to admit he'd been responsible for the second death, we couldn't stop him telling us how clever he'd been, relating every single detail, just as he did at lunch. Entirely forgetting it hadn't been very clever to allow himself to get caught out." He stopped, drank some of his wine, then said, "What was it you wanted to ask outside just before I had to leave for the station?"

Darina's feeling of unease returned. "Have you worked out how Charles managed to slip and so"—she swallowed hard—"stick the knife into Digby?"

William looked at her curiously. "No, it's not something we've given a lot of thought to yet."

"I think it was a nutmeg."

"A nutmeg?"

Darina told him how she had spilled the box of spices and of the discovery of the lone little nut by the investigating team.

William laughed. "So that was how such a small man could stab such a big one in the heart! Originally we'd thought it could only be done if Digby Cary was sitting down, otherwise it would take someone of nearly the same height to manage it."

"Which is why you were so interested in me?"

"One of the reasons." William looked at her more closely. "There's something worrying you, isn't there?" He paused, then said, "You can't possibly be thinking yourself responsible for Cary's death?"

"I did spill that box of spices and I did miss that nut. And there's Miss Makepeace as well."

"You mean you feel responsible for feeding her milk laced with sleeping pills?"

"Wouldn't you? But it's not only that. If I'd probed a bit further during our conversation in the bar last night, I'd have found out what she saw on Friday night and Charles would have known it was no use killing her."

"So, you're considering yourself as almost a murderer?" William was at his most prosaic. "Let's look at the facts. First of all, the nutmeg. Yes, if you'd picked that up, Charles Childe would not have slipped. But he might have stuck the knife into your cousin anyway. Consider also that Cary could have helped you pick up the spices and removed the nut himself. Also, if he hadn't written that review,

or hadn't laughed, Charles would not have been goaded into picking
up the knife. There's a certain ironic justice there, you know."

"Those who live by the knife and fork and all that?"

"I was thinking more of an excess of appetite—but let's go on to
Miss Makepeace. We can all look back on our careers and point to
instances where we made mistakes that had disastrous consequences. Sometimes it was through carelessness, sometimes stupidity, sometimes, like you, through the best of intentions. You were
trying to reassure Miss Makepeace, make it easy for her to give her
statement to us." He looked at her speculatively. "If she had come to
us immediately and told us the full story, no matter how confusing it
sounded, she would be alive today. But, like you, she didn't trust us
to cope with unlikely details!"

Darina drew herself up. "And what good would it have done if I
had told you my theory? Charles could easily have denied saying he'd
seen the tart, there was no proof and it was quite obvious you both
had strong suspicions about my involvement in each murder. It
would have sounded as though I was trying to cast doubt on someone else!"

"Maybe Grant was a bit hard on you," he acknowledged dryly.

"Hard on me! He accused me of murder!"

"Here's something for you to think about instead," said William
hastily. "Consider that it was I who interrupted Childe listening to
your conversation with Miss Makepeace in the bar last night more or
less at the moment he learned she'd seen something over the banisters. If *I'd* recognised his behaviour as suspicious then, maybe she
would still be alive."

Darina looked at him and he returned her regard steadily.

"Thank you," she said. After a moment she added, "I suppose we
shall never know exactly what she saw."

"From what Childe said, I assumed she saw him drag himself up
from the bottom stair just before the front door opened and the dog
came in. It wouldn't have meant much to her at the time but thinking about it afterwards, in the light of the murder investigations, she
must have realised he couldn't have been going downstairs, as he
claimed, but coming up."

"And initially that detail must have been overshadowed by her
feeling of guilt at not going down when the dog attacked," said

Darina, thinking aloud. "Perhaps if I'd got up immediately I heard the fracas, I'd have seen her."

"You're not to start on that line again," William interjected quickly. "How much are you going to miss your cousin?"

"It's strange, so much has gone on since he was killed, I think I've adjusted to his death; it's as though it all happened a long time ago. It may be different when I get away from here, though, when I go to his house."

"Ah, yes, the house. You're a lady of property now. Will you live in it?"

Darina saw the elegant Chelsea home with its charming furniture, so inseparable from her memories of Sarah. "I don't think I'll be able to afford to. My income isn't sufficient and I don't suppose Digby's estate will add much, he always spent money like there was no tomorrow."

"There'll be his royalties," pointed out William. "I believe the death of an author always creates an upsurge in sales."

Darina suddenly thought of something. "I shall make his publishers issue a new edition of the pastry book, with Miss Makepeace's name on it as well as his. I'm sure it wasn't entirely her work but she certainly deserves to be credited as co-author."

William looked at the tall girl perched on the bar stool, her long fair hair hanging so neatly down her back. "You could sell the house to finance a hotel," he suggested.

"I hadn't thought of that." Excitement lit Darina's eyes. "Do you think it would work?"

"I think anything you set your mind to would work."

Darina allowed dreams of country house hotels, furnished in splendour, lying in rural peacefulness, to drift before her inward gaze. "It would be a nice change from cooking in a different kitchen every day," she said wistfully.

"You don't think all this emphasis on food is a little dangerous?"

"Dangerous?"

"Surely it was food that raised all the passions this weekend and produced two murders?"

"It had nothing to do with it." Darina was indignant. "Charles could have been in"—she thought rapidly—"in furniture, with Digby a big noise in the antiques world and the result could have been exactly the same."

William looked politely disbelieving and said nothing.

"Perhaps a love of food does encourage certain excesses of appetite," Darina acknowledged reluctantly.

William smiled. "You know," he said, "you have an excellent detecting instinct!"

Darina was startled. "I have?"

"All you need now is a sense of teamwork. We could have set up that tart confrontation together. In the event it worked extremely well but if Charles hadn't been so taken aback and collapsed like that, we might have been able to help. Next time keep us in the picture."

Darina regarded him with a steady gaze. "That, I promise you, was my one and only excursion into detecting. I never, ever, want to have anything to do with crime, murder or the police again."

"That's a pity, I was going to ask you out to dinner. Thought I'd come up to town and you could suggest somewhere good to eat."

Darina laughed. "All right, as long as you promise not to talk about detecting or make pointed comments about food."

"Cross my heart," William said solemnly. He got up. "I have to clear up our papers. I'll be in touch in a few days, I have your number."

Darina remembered all the details she'd been asked for at the start of the investigation. Police undoubtedly had an advantage when it came to getting hold of information. She followed him out of the bar, checked nothing was left in the kitchen, and went to her car.

She got in then sat for a moment, letting the peace of the garden enfold her like a silken shawl. The traumas of the weekend fell away and into focus came an awareness of herself. Digby had left her more than a house. She recognised a new confidence, a sharpened appetite for life. A sudden sense of freedom filled her. Never before had so many possibilities beckoned. Darina started the engine, let in the clutch and moved smoothly down the drive.